*A DOUBLE MONSTER FEATURE*

# Cat People

by Peter Grandbois

&

# Dream Memories of the Fifty Foot Woman

by Irena Dubrovna

TWICE THE TERROR!
TWICE THE THRILLS!
TWICE THE MYSTERY!

SPUYTEN DUYVIL

NEW YORK CITY

# Cat People

Peter Grandbois

*The world is a cage for a woman, and inside it the woman is her own cage.*
 —Randall Jarrell


*But I welcome the darkness where the two eyes of that soft panther glow.*
 —Clarice Lispector


*I speak the way I speak inside. Not with the voice intent on sounding human, but with the other one, the one that insists I'm still a creature of the forest.*
 —Alejandra Pizarnik

Though characters from "real life" appear in this work, it is a work of fiction. Names, characters, places, and incidents are either products of the author's imagination or used fictitiously. Any resemblance to real events, fictional events (especially those in either Cat People movie) or actual persons, living or dead, specifically Nastassja Kinski, Simone Simon, and the author himself is intentional. The author will be thrilled if you believe he has somehow captured or reflected the reality of these "real" people, especially if you believe he's actually found a way to fix his own constantly shifting self to the page. That said, it is still a work of fiction. And in the end, these are still fictional characters. So, don't get too worked up about it.

The book was inspired by the author's decades long obsession with both the 1942 and the 1982 versions of Cat People. If you haven't seen the films, the author suggests you do so immediately, in whichever order you prefer. In addition, the author would also like to acknowledge a debt to both Laird Hunt's The House in the Dark of the Woods, whose title he had fun riffing on throughout the novel, and Olga Ravn's My Work, which gave the author courage to play. Finally, the line on page 202 attributed to Irena that says, "A free woman in an unfree society will become a monster," comes from Angela Carter's The Sadeian Woman and the Ideology of Pornography.

I first saw Irena Dubrovna at the rehearsal dinner, the night before her wedding. I recognized her immediately because I had been her. In some ways, I will always be her. And I will never be her again. The cute button nose and sparkling eyes promising full attention to any man who turns her way. The innocent smile we're taught to wear. The smile that never leaves, no matter what's said. No matter what she's thinking. Watch how she hangs on every word of her fiancé, Oliver, laughing at all the right moments. The perfect tilt of her head. How demure. The wide eyes, as if he's all that matters in the world. What a performance! Totally unaware she's alone on a boat at night without wind. It took me half a lifetime to rid myself of those mannerisms, the subtle gestures and looks we acquire before we learn to walk. I suppose we never fully rid ourselves of them. I sometimes catch a glimpse of myself in the mirror and see the ghost of that shy down-turned face, that sweet smile that promises so much more.

Even now, as the men stare at me, wondering who is this woman across from us, dining alone. This woman with severe, feline eyes, graying hair tied up in a black bow. This woman they do not want to know because she's of a certain age. This woman they fear because she might lead them into winter. Into hands and legs tied together. Into night's congealed blood. Even now, I fight the urge to give them what they want.

My presence disturbs them because it reminds them of their own mortality. And worse. It reminds them of the precariousness, the uncertainty, of their control. They'd like nothing more than for me to leave. So, I play with them. A little cat and mouse. I take my time as I rise from my chair, grab my purse and shawl. I watch as they turn their attention back to safer topics like who's likely to win the sweet sixteen, or what investments will net them the best return, or which car maker has the strongest reliability to cost of repair ratio. I wait before moving, wanting to give them that false sense of relief, and then I approach the wedding party. The men react first, of course. They've already marked me. One of them reaches for his fork, as if on instinct. Another tightens his grip around the young woman at his side. Another sets down his wine glass a little too quickly and spills a few drops. The red wine circles across the white tablecloth. The women who are old enough to know, spot me next. Each and every one has at one point or other in their lives squared off against the animal inside and made their choice. The reminder of who or what I am just as much a threat to them as the traitorous bruise that slowly reveals itself over the coming days on the forearm where he grabbed them. Only the younger ones keep talking, eyes fixed on their lovers, the ones, like Irena, who do not yet know themselves and of what they are capable.

It's only when I stand directly before her that she turns to me. I catch the glimmer of recognition in her eyes, though she remains unconscious of it. She pulls her napkin to her chest, holds it there like a shield. Oliver pulls her close, readies himself to step between us if necessary, as if I was a threat he had any power against.

"Meine schwester," I say, almost a whisper at first. I take a step closer, note how she crosses herself, how he starts to rise from the table. "Meine schwester," I repeat, this time loud enough for all to hear. I wait to see how the words echo inside her like a bone map, like a hunter gutting the carcass of its prey. I wait until I see the change in the cast of her eye, how it fills with a knowledge she will need to reckon with. I wait until she nearly drowns in that knowledge, and then I walk out, the collective sigh of relief in the room rushing through the door to the restaurant as it slams shut behind me.

The tableau inside reminds me of too many rooms I've been in before. I lug my own history with me from block to block as I walk back to my apartment. At times the weight is almost too much. At times, I fear I will fall beneath it and at last be free. Why? Why do questions weigh on me as if I were a child again. I thought I was past all this. Are we ever? The girl I was sitting in that restaurant, and now I carry her back with me. The girl whose father molested her and her sister, whose father made their home a living nightmare. He's dead now, but I wish he wasn't. I wanted to be the one to put him away. To see him grow old behind bars. And then, there I am again in my mind's eye. The girl who appeared topless in her first film at age thirteen. The girl who endured the flirtation and yes, the thick, probing hands, the cutting breath of her forty-three-year-old director at fifteen. The girl known worldwide at age twenty for the Vogue cover of a Burmese Python coiled around her nude body. The girl who thought sex was a game played upon her. The girl who the world thought it could play. Why do I still carry that girl within me when she'd been set free by Simone so many decades ago? But we're never really free, are we? We carry the cage inside us. We carry ourselves inside the cage.

It was 1981 in L.A. just after the Vogue cover. I was dining with my current lover, a man not worthy of a name. A man who thought what it meant to be a man was to control a much younger woman. And I was eager to be controlled. We sat opposite each other in a restaurant not that much different than the one in which I'd just left, the one in which I'd spotted my sister. Only now it was my turn.

She was an old woman by that point, seventy-one if a day. She no longer appeared in movies and rarely went out. When she did, it was always alone, usually at night. I hadn't noticed her. I admit it. All my attention wasted on my nameless lover. She caught me off guard when she spoke, "Ma soeur," she said with that French accent that became so famous. Then she repeated it. "Ma soeur. Your longing to be longed for will be your undoing." Her dress was sequined black, the kind of thing you'd only find in those old movies. A black fur stole wrapped about her shoulders.

"Who the hell are you?" my nameless lover stood. Even then, I could tell if she wanted she could cut him with a swipe of her hand. He who was everything to me was nothing to her.

"We know the waking body," she continued as if he didn't exist. "We know our own vastness."

With those words, my nameless lover sat down, vacant eyed. I started to shake, my body convulsing until I thought I would break. My nameless lover tried to hold me, to quell the shaking, but no matter how tightly he held, I couldn't stop. "What have you done to her?" he kept repeating, though he now seemed afraid to look her in the eye.

The woman simply smiled. "Her girl self is unfolding," she said, then left. The moment she turned her back, I slumped in my chair, exhausted. She'd released me. I thought at the time she'd released me from her spell. But no, that was not it at all. She'd released me from myself.

That night I had the strangest dreams. Lush, green forests and dark, fog-shrouded bayous where the branches of trees hung down toward the still water. I knew the names of things there. I understood things as if seeing them for the first time.

The moment I laid eyes on Irena I knew she was the one for me. I'd been passing the afternoon at the Lincoln Park Zoo as was my habit on Saturday afternoons when I caught sight of her standing before the leopard cage. She was drawing them. The first thing I noticed was how focused she was on every movement of those cats. She wasn't going to miss a thing. I approached, standing just to the side of her a few feet away, but she didn't acknowledge me.

"Excuse me," I said. "I couldn't help but notice you're an artist, and a beautiful one at that."

A corny opening line, I admit. And not particularly original. She didn't turn. And I don't think it was because of what I said. It was as if I didn't exist. I must have watched her for the next fifteen minutes as she sketched, never taking her eyes from those cats. Every fibre of her being focused on that one thing, almost as if they were her prey. When she closed her sketchbook, she looked up and her legs wobbled like she was going woozy. That's when I grabbed her.

For a moment, I thought she might strike me. A darkness flashed behind her eyes. But just as quickly it was gone. Replaced by a smile that cut straight to the bone. "Thank you," she said as she looked up at me from within my arms.

"You saved me a nasty fall."

She dropped her sketchbook. Looking back now, I wonder if it was an accident or a trap. I set her upright and grabbed it for her, dusting it off on my jacket. "You've got to be good," I said. "I've never seen anyone focus that intently."

"Oh," she laughed, like a flight of birds. It carried me away. "The cats always do that to me. I sketch them every time I come here."

"How often is that?"

"Any chance I get," she said, taking the sketchbook from me, holding it close, as if she feared me seeing her work.

And that's when she changed. Not that I was aware of it at the time. Only looking back from a distance can I see it. The eyes opening wider. The angelic smile to lure me in. Only after knowing what transpired, how it all came to a tragic end do I see how quickly she took over the dance I initiated. Oh, not in an overt way. Not in any way an observer could see. You couldn't put your finger on what shifted because it wasn't just one thing. It was everything. And it was as natural as the daily shift in the tide, as natural as the sound of death, and as difficult to see.

Before I knew it, I was walking her to her apartment. I'd suggested it, I thought. Though I couldn't remember saying the words. It turned out we had a lot in common. She'd wanted to become an architect as well at one point, though in the end she'd done an MFA in studio art. She liked animals, preferred cats over dogs, the same as me. And we both had a taste for music that was not part of the grunge scene that had become so popular.

When we got to her apartment, I thought I would leave, but she invited me up for coffee. It surprised me. The forwardness didn't fit in with the girlish charm. And she seemed embarrassed about it almost as soon as she'd said it.

"I mean, only if you want to," she said as if to qualify the question. "I know we've only just met, but . . ."

"I'd love to," I replied, saving her from making up a reason when we both knew we felt something. We wanted to get to know each other better. We wanted it to begin here, knowing whatever it was between us would take shape in this moment.

Her apartment was small, not much bigger than a studio. And sparsely furnished. "I don't need much," she said. "I like to spend most of my time outside."

"Difficult in the winter in Chicago," I replied, and we both laughed, then she placed her sketchbook on the coffee table and went to the kitchen.

"This is not my home," she said. "I mean, I grew up here, but it's not where I belong." She paused, as if thinking about saying more, then asked, "How do you like your coffee?"

"A little milk would be great." I couldn't stop staring at

her sketchbook. I don't know why I wanted to look inside it, but the feeling was overwhelming. "Where do you belong?" I asked, as I took the book, opened it.

She didn't respond.

"Where do you belong?" I repeated, perhaps hoping that if I could keep her talking, it would slow the moment, give me time. I wasn't prepared for the first page. I don't know what I expected. Drawings of cats, I suppose. But on the first page. And the second. And the third. And several pages after that were rough sketches of women, at first with snakes in their hair. Of course, I recognized Medusa. I'd learned about her in high school, maybe a little in college, too. How she was known for her beauty until she was raped by Poseidon in Athena's temple. How Athena punished her instead of Poseidon, turning her into a monster. I remember my college teacher making a big deal out of that detail in particular. But it's all I remembered. Anyway, the sketches were originally done in charcoal. Fairly rough. And at first, they portrayed the traditional Medusa, a woman with snakes for hair. But then, there were sketches of a woman with leopards crawling out of her hair, all claws and teeth. And in the most recent sketches, which were done in pencil and in reds and blacks, the leopards seemed to emerge from the women's head, almost as if they were birthed there, then they proceeded to eat her. The most recent sketches were unusually detailed, disturbingly so, with the big cats eviscerating the woman whose head already lay in pieces. I shut the notebook just as she returned with our coffee.

"I don't know where I belong," she said. "It's strange because I think about it all the time. Somewhere warmer. That much I know." She smiled again, that angelic smile. I couldn't reconcile the smile with the drawings I'd just seen.

She sat closer to me than I expected. Though I didn't mind. And we talked longer than either of us had hoped. We talked well into the night as if each of us had found not only our voice, but someone who would be a receptacle for that voice, a vessel we could pour that voice into. A vessel that would never be full. At one point, I remember touching the bones of my face, feeling as if they were water, feeling as if she'd filled me and now all that was left was to pour myself back into her. And that's when it happened.

I leaned over to kiss her. The moment felt right. I was sure she was ready. She was willing. She leaned in as well. Her lips parting. Eyes closing. Her sweet breath dusting my lips. And then suddenly an impenetrable darkness stretched between us. There's no other way to describe it. It was as if I could no longer reach her, and she couldn't reach me no matter how hard we tried. As I opened my eyes, I caught her blowing gently twice on each wrist, then she stood, started to make an excuse. "I'm sorry, I don't know why I did that. I like you. I really do."

I stood, took her hands in mine. Her skin smoother, more delicate than any I'd ever felt. "I understand," I said. "Things have moved very fast." I tried to laugh, to make light of the situation. "I promise. I'm usually much slower. Turtle slow in fact. Usually, women dump me because I take too long to make the first move."

She laughed then. A delicate sound like bells jingling. "You're funny . . . and cute," she said. "A dangerous combination."

Discretion is the better part of valor, so I made my way to the door. "Will I see you again?" I asked.

She brought her hands to her chest, hesitated, as if my question had startled her, as if she hadn't thought of what might come next. Had I not known better, I could have sworn fear shadowed the cheekbones of her face and limned her eyes. At the time, I blew it off, thinking she seemed so innocent in the ways of love and that I'd come on too strong. I've never understood women particularly well and Irena least of all. I wish I could say I came to a true understanding, even if late in our relationship, but that would be a lie.

We dated over the next few months. At first just once a week, but very quickly it turned to twice a week, then three times, then nearly every night. So, when I received the job offer to join a prestigious architectural firm in L.A., I asked her to marry me. She kissed me. It wasn't the first time we'd kissed. We'd kissed before, but those kisses always felt restrained. Close mouthed. It's not that this kiss was all that different. Still frustratingly close mouthed. But this time, she released a groan, almost like an animal, and pressed her pelvis to mine. It must have shocked her, as she pulled away almost as quickly as it happened and blew twice on each wrist in the way I'd come to know.

# ALICE

The world is a hollow longing. At least in my book. But nobody wants to talk about it. We just go on pretending. We long to be longed for. And yet, how rarely is that longing reciprocated. Oh sure, I can make you want me. I know how to do that. I know how to do it well, in fact. Most women do. I can dress the part. Show just enough leg. Just enough cleavage. Wear my hair a certain way. Paint my eyes a certain way. Walk a certain way. But it's not real. I get your attention. I rouse your lust. Maybe that turns to something more. Maybe it leads to a relationship where I shift to a different sort of performance. But the longing never goes away.

Maybe that's what fascinated me about Irena. She didn't seem to understand the performance. She seemed, at times, to have no idea about it. Most kids kept their distance from her as a result, and I admit, I kept my distance too. But I watched. I couldn't help it. She seemed so different from everything I'd known, everything I'd thought I understood with her simple white blouses and plaid skirts. Her lack of makeup. The fact that she didn't shave her legs. I mean she didn't shave! The way she walked on the balls of her feet as if she were almost running. She didn't even seem to understand how best to tie back her hair so it would at least sway suggestively when she walked so fast. Kids like that in junior high usually disappear from the radar of others. But for some reason, it locked her onto mine. That and what happened the first time I saw her.

We were sitting in Ms. Hahn's math class. Irena sat in front. I was in the back. Irena must have known. I mean she must have. In my experience, you feel the cramps. You know it's coming on. Maybe it was her first time. I don't know. She could have asked to go to the bathroom. I don't know why she didn't. She couldn't have been afraid of Ms. Hahn. She wasn't one of those teachers who refused bathroom privileges or who gave you a lecture about the difference between "can" and "may" when you asked, *Can I go to the bathroom? I don't know, can you?* But for some reason she didn't go. She sat frozen in her seat. Danny Collins was the first to notice the blood dripping down her leg. He whispered the monstrous fact to Martha Wilkinson, who spread the news to Cecily Twichell and so on down the line. Remarkably, no one cried out for Ms. Hahn. No one stopped the class, which made it all the worse, I think, for Irena. They simply pointed and gossiped behind the teacher's back. Irena heard them. She must have. But she never turned around. Didn't acknowledge them in the slightest. She only blew twice on each wrist then continued clinging to her desk. When the bell rang, she stayed frozen in her seat, which was how I knew she had to know what had happened. It didn't matter though. We all knew the bottom of her skirt would be stained red. We'd already seen the blood stuck to the hairs on her unshaven legs. I can't imagine what it was like for her walking down the hallways between classes the rest of the day. It only takes one incident like that in junior high to mark you as an outsider for the rest of your life. But that wasn't the only time it happened. And it wasn't the only thing that marked her as different from her peers.

Irena was smart. If she didn't have the problems she clearly had, she could have been class valedictorian. And smart and weird are two things you don't want to be as a teenager. She was particularly good in English, had her hand raised usually before Mr. Browne could even finish his questions. How she could understand Shakespeare was beyond me. Didn't she know she already had enough of the wrong kind of attention. How could she not understand? In my world, you learned quickly You had to be very careful. You certainly didn't act smart even if you were. You didn't do things that made you stand out. You dressed like everyone else, which in the early 2000's meant low-rise jeans, pop-corn tops, and UGG boots. And, of course, a flip phone. Irena didn't have any of that.

"Going unnoticed" meant you did exactly what you needed to do to get "noticed," but only "noticed enough."

You never wanted "too much notice." So, for a girl, "going unnoticed" meant smiling at the right people (boys), laughing at the right time (jokes told by boys), dressing to be "noticed just enough" (by boys and other girls), but not dressing to be "noticed too much" (by boys and other girls), knowing when to be nice and when to shut up, and never ever raising your hand in class. To be unnoticed sans quotations meant you were marked. It meant you were noticed and labeled deficient. It meant you were talked about in ways you didn't want to be talked about. Irena was unnoticed.

By the time you got to high school, "going unnoticed" meant knowing who to date and that you better be seeing someone whether you wanted to or not. "Going unnoticed" meant you dated the varsity linebacker, as I did. Not the quarterback. That got you noticed. "Going unnoticed" meant you were a pom pon girl and not a cheerleader. You did not participate in choir or band, and you certainly were not a thespian. "Going unnoticed" meant you went only to the right parties and drank only enough to "go unnoticed." If you drank too much you quickly became very, very noticed. If you drank too much you often ended up in an upstairs bedroom with someone you wouldn't remember. If you drank too much, you quickly became "a slut." You became "that girl." And no one wanted to be "that girl."

Irena seemed to go out of her way to get noticed. I'll never forget that afternoon in the early weeks of sex education, the class in which every student understands intuitively you don't ask questions if you want to "go unnoticed." Irena raised her hand just as Ms. Dillbone finished her lecture on female sexuality, labia majora vs labia minora, etc. "Yes, Ms. Dubrovna." Ms. Dillbone always called us by our last names.

"When you masturbate, is it normal for your nails to grow long and sharp, and for hair to grow on your arms?" Irena asked as if she were from a different planet, as if she had no idea how this would make her unnoticed in the worst possible way, meaning very, very noticed.

To her credit, Ms. Dillbone didn't bat an eye. Only the slightest twitching of her upper lip gave any indication she was surprised by the question at all. She pondered it for a long moment, staring at Irena as if trying to determine if she was serious. Irena stared back wide-eyed. "That sounds like one of the things I was told when I was young," Ms. Dillbone replied. "I distinctly remember the nuns at my school, you see I went to a catholic school. And I'll never forget the nuns telling me if I masturbated I would go blind, or grow hair on my hands, or worse, go to hell. It is simply not true, Irena." Ms. Dillbone looked proud of the honesty behind her answer, as if she'd been waiting a lifetime for that moment, proud at least until the class erupted in fits and giggles. Then she had her job cut out for her quieting us down. Of course, Irena's hand was up again almost immediately. "Yes, Irena," Ms. Dillbone said, a hint of impatience in her voice, as she knew any follow up was bound to lead to further class disruptions.

"But it *is* true," Irena said. "My fingernails do grow long and sharp . . ."

"Perhaps you should clip them." Ms. Dillbone curtly replied, perhaps thinking that Irena was trying to cause trouble and not that she could have possibly been serious. The class burst into laughter, and all Irena heard for weeks in the halls after were calls to *Cut your nails!*

The incident also led to Paul Parks stealing Irena's backpack when she was walking home from school that afternoon. Rumors flew quickly after that. *Brad says he found a couple sex books in there. He says one of the books was about a sex dungeon where people did S & M. (Most of us had no idea what S & M was but that didn't stop the rumors.) He says she'd underlined the parts where people were tied up and where they got spanked. He says there were a lot of dog-eared pages.*

What more can I say? I tried my best to guide her, to drop hints. It didn't matter. After that, Irena became the poster child for going unnoticed.

# Dr. Louis Judd



Note: Patient exhibits acute anxiety. She is a beautiful woman to be sure, though she makes little attempt to be beautiful. No makeup. She wore a skirt to our first session and I noticed immediately her unshaven legs. I'm not sure if this is a conscious defiance of social norms or an unconscious result of her anxiety. She is thin, perhaps to a fault. When sitting, she tends to hunch, as if hiding something, or as if uncomfortable with her own body. Fifteen minutes into the session, the patient said, "I like to be liked."

I asked her, "What does it mean to you to be liked? Patient sat for a long moment, hands reaching for her purse, then settling in her lap before answering. "It means that someone or something wants to be with me, to spend time with me, to be close to me." She stared out the window while answering, all the while watching a robin bouncing from branch to branch in the oak outside my office.

"And what do you do to make it so someone wants to be with you?"

She turned to me, surprised at the question. "What do you mean by that?"

"I simply mean do your actions push people away or draw them to you?" The question clearly agitated her. She rubbed her right thumb against her right forefinger repeatedly. Again, she stared out the window, though the robin was gone now.

"I try to be nice," she said. "I do everything I can to be nice." She looked down at her lap. "But it never works out for me. Even now, I can see Oliver getting tired, getting frustrated. He's already questioning whether he really loves me. And we've been married only a few months." She reached for the Kleenex box I keep on the end table as if to pre-empt the tears that glimmered in her eyes.

"What makes you say that? How do you know? Have you asked him?"

Patient thought about this for a long moment.

"I don't need to ask him." She looked at me then. The first direct eye contact of the session. "I can see it in the way he looks at me."

"What do you mean?"

Note: Patient showed typical signs of increased agitation, i.e., leg shaking, erratic breathing.

"He bought me a kitten."

"Most people would see getting a present as a sign of love."

"He bought it for me because we aren't intimate. I won't let him close." Her attention moved from me to the Kleenex box beside her.

"Let's table the intimacy question for the moment. Again, I ask, how do you know? Did you ask him why he bought the kitten?"

"I didn't need to." She grabbed the Kleenex box and pulled it to her lap. "I just knew."

"It seems you are making assumptions without actually asking him what he's thinking."

"The cat didn't like me!" she said, squashing the Kleenex box in her lap. "It wouldn't go near me. And if I tried to touch it, the thing just hissed at me. He took the kitten back to the pet shop and exchanged it for a canary."

Her sudden emotion surprised me. She clearly attempts to present with a calm demeanor, and this affectation is largely successful, but there are ripples beneath this calm surface. "It sounds like your husband is a very thoughtful man." I chose my words carefully, tossing my line into the depths of that calm water. What might it pull up?

Note: Patient's eyes narrowed. Where she was agitated before, she put on a forced smile. Hands still clenching the squashed Kleenex box.

"Yes, he is thoughtful, isn't he. Such a nice man. I don't know where I'd be without him."

I'd hit the target. But just as quickly as a hint of real emotion emerged, the patient's voice became flat, as if she were retreating inside herself. I would have to work very hard with this one.

"Do you have a problem with him being thoughtful?"

"No." Her reply was quick. Firm. Then she paused as if considering. "It's just that I didn't want a bird. I wanted to be liked, to be loved. By him. Do you see? By him. Not by a bird."

"Wasn't the act of giving you a gift an act of love?"

"Perhaps."

Note: Patient began slowly shredding the Kleenex box in her lap as she talked. My probing was getting closer to the mark. I did not know then, just how many marks would prove false ones.

"The bird seemed fine in its cage, away from me. Doing what birds do, chirping and singing. But once Oliver was gone at work, I felt lonely. Incredibly alone. I only wanted to touch the bird. To feel something. Some contact. I opened the cage door and reached inside. The bird squawked and flew away from my hand. I tried again, but the bird grew frantic, screaming as it flew repeatedly into the top of the cage. I didn't stop. I couldn't stop. I tried to grab it, but the moment I touched it, the bird fell to the cage floor, dead."

Note: Patient seemed oblivious to the Kleenex box torn and scattered about her feet. She rose and walked to the window, staring out. I would have to be careful with my next steps.

"Have you ever heard of *Thanatos*, the death drive?" She didn't answer or turn from the window. "It's funny, you know, Freud got the credit for that one, but the theory actually originated with a woman named Sabina Spielrein, a student of Jung's. A student who later became his lover. Freud simply capitalized on Sabina's work. I don't suppose you're interested in the history of psychology."

Note: Again, she did not respond. Her lack of response, her clear attempt to disassociate from what I said seemed more evidence of her unwillingness to connect, or her fear of where that connection might lead.

"The death drive is an instinct of destruction set against the external world, but not always."

She turned from the window. "I'm sorry, Dr. Judd, but what does this have to do with wanting to be liked, to be loved?"

"*Thanatos* and *Eros*, the death drive and the need for love, the need to love, are always in opposition. "I don't know what happened to the bird. I don't what to speculate, but perhaps your need to be loved is pushing your husband away."

"What are you talking about?"

It was then the patient became aware of the torn Kleenex box, the shredded tissues all over the floor. "I'm so sorry," she said. "What have I done? I don't see how I could have done such a thing." She knelt on the floor, frantically picking up the tissues. "You must forgive me doctor. This is really not like me. I'm so sorry."

"There's nothing to forgive, Irena. And no need to clean up. I'll take care of it when our session is over." She didn't stop. I'm not even sure she heard me, and so I waited.

Note: Patient increased the pace at which she was picking up the shredded Kleenex. Once she gathered all the pieces, she stuffed them in her purse, as if she didn't want to bother me by putting the pieces in my trash.

"Do I have your attention now, Irena?"

"Yes, of course, doctor." She turned her head to me but kept her gaze to the floor, scanning still for a tissue she may have missed.

I took a chance and went on anyway. "I'm simply saying that it seems your husband wants to love you, that he wants to connect with you. Why are you not allowing it to happen?

What are you afraid of?" Perhaps it was too pointed. Perhaps I'd let my frustration get the better of me. She stood silent, as if the cat had her tongue.

"If you don't like Freud," I said. "Maybe you'd agree with the psycho-analyst Jacque Lacan. He thought that Freud was wrong, that there was no war between *Eros* and *Thanatos*. Lacan thought that everything was the death drive, that everything pursues its own extinction, every drive involves the subject in an endless cycle of repetition, every drive is an attempt to go beyond *Eros*, to the realm where enjoyment is experienced as suffering."

Note: Patient's knees buckled. Thankfully, I was quick to respond and caught her before she fell. I settled her back on the couch and brought her smelling salts, which seemed to do the trick. I must admit, her own wild smell caught me off-guard. The flash of her eyes when they opened. For a moment, I was almost afraid. Almost enchanted. She immediately blew twice on each wrist, then looked at me as if ashamed.

"You are a complex woman, Irena, with many walls, many anxieties keeping whoever is the real Irena at bay. Who are you, Irena Dubrovna? Who are you?"

Again, her eyes flashed. She looked as if she might hit me.

"I'm sorry," I said, scratching my head, not unaware of

the fact that my hand rose as a defensive gesture. "Perhaps I've been too direct for this early in our relationship." Frustration colored my words. It seemed we were finished with this session. "Do you have anything more you'd like to add before we wrap up?" I stepped away, putting some distance between myself and her.

She opened her mouth, but no words came out. Then, a voice as if from deep inside. "Mother never learned to swim," she said, softly, with little variation in intonation, almost like an obedient child. "She was afraid of the water. Father made sure we never traveled anywhere near large bodies of water. No lakes. No oceans. Only inland for us. After she was gone, Father showed us how to sift flour, how to make eggs, how to cook."

"I'm sorry, Irena, where are you going with this?" I put down my pad and pencil, signaling to her that her time was up.

"I still can't go near the water," she replied, turning to me with sunken eyes. "When it rains, I can't go outside. The long, red worms slither up from the ground."

"I fail to see the connection, Irena. Are you saying, the worms, too, have a death drive, that they die when they seek the hope of the surface?"

"I'm saying they die either way."

# PETER

It's 1982. You're eighteen. Boy or girl. Okay. Boy. Fine, but it doesn't really matter. All that matters is that you're finally sitting in the middle of the third row in the mall theatre, about to watch *Cat People*, starring Nastassja Kinski and Malcolm McDowell. You've been burning for this moment since you saw the movie trailer with the David Bowie soundtrack, the trailer that teased a woman coming of age, a woman waiting to be told what to do, who she was, with each scene:

*The white blouse hanging in the window under a full moon. Cut to Irena lying in bed, sheets pulled up over her naked body. Cut to Irena walking an empty room in a white suit like someone possessed, a strange wind blowing her red scarf behind her. Cut to a passionate kiss between Irena and her lover, Oliver. She backs away, frightened. Cut to her brother played by Malcolm McDowall telling Irena, "Make love to me," as they superimpose the legs of a leopard walking through the desert. Cut to Irena shot from behind. She strips off her clothing piece by piece as she walks up the stairs. As she pulls off her blouse, we see she wears no bra. Cut to Irena and her lover in bed, kissing. Her nails grow sharp and tear through the sheets. Cut to Irena walking through the desert in the same white suit as before, the same red scarf. The scarf blowing in the wind. Cut to her brother telling her only he can help her escape this nightmare. Cut to scenes of hunting cats with nets, with guns, men walking through the forest, Irena crouching catlike, ready to pounce.*

You don't know what it is about the trailer, maybe it's the allure of the tagline, "an erotic fantasy about the animal in us all." Maybe it's the promise of Nastassja Kinski's slightly parted, full lips. Maybe it's the short, boyish haircut that combined with her ultra-slim body gives her a sort of androgynous appeal. Maybe it's the way she walks through those scenes that sometimes appear to be in a desert, sometimes an empty, white room, those scenes where she wears the schoolgirl's white dress with the mysterious red scarf, the red scarf that calls to mind Little Red Cap from the Brothers' Grimm.

The trailer struck something in you. Something that burned for months as you waited impatiently for the movie to be released, reading every article on it that came out in the entertainment magazines you found in the mall bookstore. You learned it was a re-make, that there was another *Cat People* made in 1942, forty years earlier. Even though it's in black and white and therefore to your young mind most likely terrible you race to the video store to rent it.

The clerk, an older man with grey-flecked beard and

glasses, seems surprised by your request. Not many teenagers asking to rent old classics. He takes it as a sign that you, too, are a film aficionado. You are not.

"Some great filmmaking there," he says with a gleam in his eye. "Tourneur's use of light and shadow was way ahead of its time."

You nod in agreement, as if you have any idea what he's talking about.

Back at home, sitting alone in your basement in the dark, you are disappointed as the film ends. It certainly wasn't scary. Certainly not a horror movie. Not even a monster movie, really. Why do people keep saying "the classics" are good? You've never seen one you liked. It's back to your golden rule—if it's in black and white, it sucks. *Citizen Cane*. Blech. *The Maltese Falcon*. Come on! Your dad forced you to watch those, telling you they were "classics." And sure, they were okay, but in the end, a big disappointment.

And yet somehow the '82 Schrader re-make had you going to the mall just to stare at the movie posters promising future attractions. The fiery orange background. The left side of the poster an ancient, barren tree, black panthers lying on the lower branches, one panther standing on a rock at the base of the tree, open mouthed, perhaps growling. The right half of the poster filled with half of Nastassja Kinski's face, those full, slightly parted lips, that short, boyish haircut, the one eye we can see, colored green with the vertical pupal of a cat. The eye that seemed to look directly into what desert, what forest inside you?

At the time you wanted sex without the danger of sex. Like wanting the Barbie instead of the real woman. You loved playing with your sister's Barbies as a kid. Taking their clothes off and pressing their bodies together. Sex without sex. And now you're eighteen. A virgin. You asked your first girlfriend out when you were fifteen, not because you liked her but because everyone knew she liked you, and your friends told you that you must be gay because you didn't want a girlfriend. So, you did it. You asked her out. But you didn't kiss her. At least not until she got mad at you opening night of the play you starred in, *Bye Bye Birdie*. You played the lead. No not Conrad Birdie, the Elvis like singer. Everyone who doesn't know the play thinks that's the lead, but the real lead is his manager, the very nice, respectful, and unthreatening, Albert Peterson.

You were always nice. The same way you always wore white shirts in high school. You were careful to always say the right thing. To never ever get angry. To smile even when you were sad. You were trained that way at home where negative emotions were not allowed. But that's another story, for another time. The important thing now is that you were especially always nice with girls. You didn't want to push too far, to make them feel desire, to feel sexual. You didn't want to feel sexual. It scared you. So, you didn't kiss your girlfriend until she threw a fit behind the stage on opening night. Came up after the show not to congratulate you but to say in front of everyone with tears in her eyes, "How could you kiss her on stage before you even kissed your own girlfriend?" Of course, *Birdie* ends happily ever after with Albert finally realizing he loves his long-time friend and secretary, Rosie. After proposing to her at the end of the play, he kisses her, showing his first real passion.

You kissed your first girlfriend, right then and there, in full makeup, in front of everyone involved in the play. You kissed her to hide your shame. You'll never forget how she changed the moment you kissed her, how her entire body opened into you, the almost animal groan she released in that first sloppy kiss. The deep longing of her tongue. It was as if in that moment you existed in two worlds because all the while you kissed her, you were also keenly aware of everyone watching, as if you were still on stage and this was just another performance. You kissed her with your eyes open. And that's when you saw it, crouched in the corner of the dressing room, hunched over in the shadows behind a table filled with makeup. Slowly, it raises its head, its arm, pointing a claw-like finger with a sharp nail. It's eyes licking you.

If you think this is Irena, you're sadly mistaken. It's no more Irena than the other characters. Maybe they're more Irena than I am. I don't know. This is Irena's voice. Sure. But what does that even mean? We all have so many voices, so many people inside us. Irena is just another front for the person who wrote this book. And who is that? It's certainly not the person whose name appears on the cover. That's too easy. Too simplistic. Because of course the author is just another front. And that Peter character? Forget it. I mean, what do you want me to say? There's never just one person writing. Or at least not the person we think. So, let's just agree right now that Peter wrote this book about as much as I did (meaning Irena), or Nastassja, or Oliver, or Alice, or Dr. Judd. Let's agree that someone else wrote this book. Someone who must remain invisible. Someone who found a way to speak through the author, through these characters, through me. Of course, that creates all sorts of problems. Not the least of which is who gets paid for this book. As if this book will make any money! But it also creates problems of plotting and time. It means that however we arrange the events, that arrangement is arbitrary, that what seems like the neat and orderly progression of story is just our need to arrange things for maximum dramatic, thematic, and emotional affect. It's not necessarily how events played out at all. It has more to do with our own obsessions, our own predilections than anything else. Our need for sense. For order. Or rather, it has more to do with the needs of that someone who must remain invisible. Which may as well be me. I'm the most likely candidate. I'm the one everyone seems to be going on and on about. It's funny. I have no recollection of most of the events described here thus far. It's as if they exist in a dream. Some of them I'm not even sure actually happened. Take that in for just a second. I've been told they happened, but what does that really mean. When I try to remember them, I just draw a blank. It's like a giant black curtain falls over my brain. So maybe this whole thing is just my attempt to re-create what I don't remember, to re-arrange my life into something that I can remember, into something that makes the smallest bit of sense. Maybe it's me trying desperately to become me. Or maybe it's the many people that make up the author (who might be me) trying to become whole. I don't know. I'm not sure of anything anymore but the present moment. And because I may be fictional, I'm really not even sure of that. Maybe this book is some kind of record so I, so we, don't get lost in that present moment. Maybe this book is the author's, or that invisible someone again, attempt to be seen, if that's even possible. I mean, we don't know who we are most of the time, do we? So how can we expect someone else to know, even with a book? It would take a library of books. And it's easy to get lost in a library. I've done it, we've done it, many times. So, even then, who knows?

# NASTASSJA

After that first encounter, I dreamed of Simone. Or rather, for many nights, I dreamed I was Simone.

*Scene One:* 1931. Sitting alone in a Paris café. Rain falling.

The city grows like an unwelcome forest about me. My body eager for a change from wasted days. A hummingbird's flight carries me to another childhood, where I sit with my Italian mother on the beach. "Open your mouth you animal and speak anything," she says to me.

I growl my best growl, and she laughs and scoops me into her arms.

"You must be careful with that growl, my love," she says. Her eyes like newly coined worlds. "A growl like that can get you into trouble. A growl like that frightens people."

The orange sun sinks slowly into the sea behind her, as if swallowed by it, and I'm left staring at a man who stands looking at me in the café, a man in a pin-striped suit with stern, sterile eyes, and an arched brow.

"You are the most beautiful woman I've ever seen. So delicately pretty," he says by way of introduction. "May I sit."

I take a long sip of my cold espresso, then rise and slap the man hard across the face. He hides the shock well, turning his head back to re-appraise me, bringing his hand to his chin, massaging it. His jaw sets as if he's made up his mind. "My name is Victor," he says. "Victor Tourjansky." He offers his hand. "Innocent face. Fire underneath. I like that. And I'd like you to be in my picture, my moving picture."

I consider him. I'd been working as a model for the past two years and hated it. Being told what to do, and when and how to do it. Part your lips just so. *No.* Tilt your head this way. *No, not quite right.* Being what the camera needed you to be, what the viewer needed you to be. Would movies be any different? Doubtful. The chance to act. To be someone else. Maybe even to discover who I really am. No. It's not for me. I'm not ready.

I step back to the sand, back to my mother's arms, but when I do, I trip over a chair, and he catches me.

*Scene Two:* 1936. Hollywood. On the set of *Under Two Flags.*

"We want you to be sleeker, more glamorous, darling," my latest director, Frank, says. "Just let the wardrobe people work their magic, you'll see." He walks toward me as if he's always skipping to a beat only he hears. He reaches out, moves a loose strand of my hair back behind my ear.

I close my eyes, but it doesn't help. I can't shut this world out. I can't live inside myself. So, I'm left to become someone else. "What's wrong with what I'm wearing," I answer, looking only at his heavy eyebrows because I don't want to give him the satisfaction of looking into his eyes.

"It's just not the kind of look we're going for, darling," he says, running his hands through his own slick-backed hair. "You know what the studio execs are like. You know what they want. Come on darling, be a dear and play the game, would you?"

"I thought for once I might escape the pouty lips, the clothes that show just the right amount of hip," I say, turning away from him. "I don't know if I want to do this. If I can do this. It's not me."

"Oh, get over yourself darling," the director says. "You're a player or you wouldn't be here." I can hear him pulling the pack of cigarettes from his breast pocket. I hear the click of the lighter, smell the smoke. "I want to be naked with you, but I'm stuck here directing this miserable picture. Nobody in Hollywood really gets what they want, darling." He touches my back with one hand, reaching around me with the other, offering me the cigarette.

I slap his hand away, knocking the cigarette to the floor. The director steps away, "If that's how you want to play it, I'm certain we can replace you. I hear Claudette Colbert is available, and she's much more amenable to director's wishes. I hear she's very nice to work with."

I don't say a word. The cigarette burns on the floor, the embers like a cat's eye.

*Scene Three:* 1937. Patton State Mental Hospital, Los Angeles.

I don't know why I'm here. Why I'm tied to this bed. Why they are injecting me in my rear with 4 cc's of Metrazol. I don't want to lose the self I'm becoming. And then I'm convulsing. The nurse puts something in my mouth to keep me from biting my tongue. The doctor stands like a demon before me. A winged demon. I try to recall a name. Any name. But my only memory is pain. And time unwound to stone upon stone in my limbs, crushing them.

This is not my world. And I am not part of it. I am not their reliquary. I am not their daughter. Not their sex kitten. Their femme fatale. "Fiery tempered." "Difficult." "Temperamental." All the labels hung on me while I'm hung up to dry on the screen in whatever they want me to wear. Doing whatever they want me to do.

The machinery of my hands turns like a clock. I cannot stop them.

Look. Now. My chest is open. And that demon doctor is plucking the blue notes. I wonder, does he find who I really am. Does he find the me trapped within? My own writer, director, set designer. Does he see the lights set just so? Lights set to make me that perfect combination of innocent and dangerous. Or does he see the fallen light within my body that they put there?

Someday, I'll become what I was, what I am. What I am meant to be. No giant movie screens with my two-story face. Someday, I'll become what I want and wander the sidewalks, the restaurants, the bars and beaches. I'll carry who I am under my tongue. I'll carry it in the growl of the cat released in the night. And no one will pluck my strings for me.

And still the doctors talk. And still the nurses pedal pills. And still this ocean keeps rising, pouring into my nose, my mouth, my ears, until I can no longer hear the sunken sound of my voice, until I can no longer speak at all. And yet, the ocean is wide. And I will yet cross this season of water.

*Scene Four*: A montage from the late 1940s to 1970s. Setting shifts back and forth between France and Hollywood.

I am no longer theirs. Let them create their fictions, their tabloid stories. I will live alone in my Paris apartment. Take a lover when I want. Talk to whom I want. Eat by myself in a restaurant if I choose, and now no one thinks of approaching me to say, "You are the most beautiful woman I've ever seen." I am a woman over forty, a woman of a certain age. Invisible to the public, except for the stories the tabloids generate. But those are make believe. They aren't real, though the "reality" they create can be devastating.

*Simone's maid comes clean, saying, "She has a gold key to her boudoir she gives to any man who wants it!"*

*Simone takes Serbian double agent, Dusko Popov, as a lover!*

*The FBI file on Simone is more than an inch thick!*

*Simone has long-term affair with wealthy, married French businessman!*

Let them create their fictions, their foreign bodies. They are not mine. I will remain in the woods, searching for the city of cats. Take my walks when I want. I will grow old and die alone. But I will die with my truth intact within me.

I woke troubled from these dreams and went out to my back porch, where the cold morning air might shake me free of the thoughts stirring within. What would I become, I who had been so good at being what others wanted, at being wanted. How would I speak truth, that thin reed that can so easily be braided into a lie? How would I find her city of cats without a friend, a sister, to guide me? Simone did it on her own. She found it, I think. At least, I dreamed she found it. I had no way of knowing for sure. But that uncertainty was necessary. At least, I thought it was. I felt somehow deep inside that it was.

Now, at the edge of my life, I feel alone. That's why I've chosen this moment to speak. Are you hearing this? You, who are that friend, that sister, sent to lead me. Do you have the bone map that offers a way home? Do you hear me? How some days I want so suddenly to be naked. To walk the forest, any forest, where the air is fingerless and no longer touches my skin.

We couldn't resist each other. Night after night, softening into each other's bodies. Maybe it was because of the frustration, the fact that we never actually went all the way, that the initial sparks were so hot. I started to believe that what's most real in life is what goes unfulfilled. At least, that's what takes on the most weight and spreads across our days. All we needed, Irena and I, was that one small, impossible act. Yet somehow it eluded us.

Each night an eternity. Out at sea each night. I couldn't help feeling it was my fault, that I was unable to find a way to reach her. But then I knew that couldn't be true. We kissed. She pushed her body into mine. I held her tight. When our breath caught fire, I peeled off her clothes. Each piece of clothing a note, a song that bound us closer. We were built to live in each other. Once we were naked, I laid her down on the bed, gently, moving my hands over her body.

"I want to be a gazelle against your palm," she whispered in my ear. That's all I needed to hear. My hand moved between her legs, touching her there. She let out a moan, almost a growl.

"Was that you?" I asked. Not that I was shocked. Women have made all sorts of sounds in bed with me before. But this sound came from a different place, a deeper place. As if from a dark forest. It frightened me a little. And that's where it ended. The fire of our breath extinguished as quickly as it was ignited.

"I didn't hear anything," she said, still panting hard. "Did I make a sound?" She took my hand in hers. "All I want tonight is to make you happy.

"You do make me happy." I forced myself to look into her eyes. I wanted her to see I was sincere, but I could tell she was already receding, already moving away.

"I envy every woman I see on the street. They're happy. They make their husbands happy." She pulled my hand to her breast. "I'm tired of this body, this dance."

"I am happy. So, so happy." If I repeated it enough, I knew I could believe it. I tried again to ignite what was between us. To write on her sun-flecked body. And for a moment, she joined in, rubbing against me, pulling me closer, kissing me. And then it happened, her mouth opened slightly. It was no longer the kiss of a girl, but of a woman. I reached again between her legs, felt the wetness.

"Take me. Take me," she begged. "Let our bodies live the way they want."

I held her hands, one on each side of her head, our fingers intertwined. I looked into her eyes but found nothing there. They'd gone flat, black. Her legs parted, and I pressed myself against her. Again, she growled, holding my hands so tight I thought they might break. I froze. Just for an instant, but it was enough. She closed her legs, pushed me away from her, and sat up on the edge of the bed, her back to me.

"You think I'm a monster," is that it? she asked. "You think I want it too much?"

"Not at all, my love," I replied, moving beside her, again holding her in my arms. "It's a little strong, I admit it, but I . . ."

"You what?" she turned to me.

"I like it . . . I think."

"Only the monstrous kind of love can rearrange me," she said it as a challenge. As if she wanted me to best her. She stood before me, daring me to do something. The problem was I didn't know what to do. Strike her? Hold her? I didn't even know what to say.

She turned away, brought her hands to her face, as if she'd changed her mind, as if she were now embarrassed.

"I don't know what that means." I stood, walked to the bathroom, splashed water over my face, then returned wrapped in a towel. "What does that mean? What are you saying, darling?"

"It means I'm afraid, Oliver," she replied, turning to me. "I'm afraid of what might happen if I let my body go."

I laughed, then seeing the hurt on her face, stifled it.

"Nothing's going to happen. Except that maybe we'll both enjoy it," I said.

"Will we?" She looked at me with such hope in her eyes. "Dr Judd says pleasure and pain are the same in the end. That in seeking out love, we also desire to destroy that love. What if I hurt you?"

I started to wonder if Dr Judd was worth the money. This was frustrating, to say the least. I can't tell you how many times this exact scenario had played out. "Maybe you're asexual," I said, regretting it as soon as the words left my mouth. "Maybe you don't really like sex, and you're pretending just to please me."

She winced at that, as if I'd hit her. Then silence for a long moment. I thought about getting dressed. Giving her time alone. When she spoke again, her voice was cold, as if drawn from the bottom of a deep ocean. "I know I used to sing," she said.

"Again, I don't know what that means." I let my frustration show. "Are you saying you were able to have sex with guys before me?"

"No, Oliver," she replied, frustrated now, too, but at least sounding more human. "You know you're the first for me. I've told you that."

"Then what?"

"I used to sing in a body before this one, or maybe a

different body than this one. I don't know." She crawled onto the bed, moving around on all fours. The image of her on all fours both attracted and frightened me.

"You're not making sense, Irena. In fact, you're sounding a little crazy." Again, I regretted the words, and yet I said them.

"If I sing who I am, I'm afraid you won't like it." She stopped crawling, sitting in the center of the bed, looking at me with the widest, darkest, most beautiful eyes I'd ever seen.

"I love you, Irena. Why would I not like it?" I came to her in the center of the bed, held her once again. "Anything that comes from you I will love. How could I not?" But even as I spoke the words, I could hear the inauthenticity in my voice. Could she hear it, too? The doubt lurking at the edges. Would I love her no matter what? Does anyone really love anyone no matter what, unless, of course, they're your children. If I was honest, I was already wondering if our rapid marriage had been a good idea. I'd confided as much to Alice the other day at work.

"I'm afraid if I open to you, you won't like me. You'll think I'm a monster," she said, hiding her face in her hands. She must have been so wrapped up in her own worries, she didn't hear my lack of conviction.

"That's ridiculous." This was going too far. How much

could a man endure. It was bad enough that we'd been married for six months and still hadn't had sex. Now she was getting weird. I wasn't into weird. It wasn't part of my vocabulary.

"I'm strange to this language," she went on. "I speak it so as not to be alone." She stood, separated herself from me, as if she feared my rejection. She paced back and forth in front of the bed, looking as if she was trapped, as if she were behind bars.

"I know your parents were from Serbia, but I thought you were born here. I thought English was your native language." I stood as well, grabbed my pants, my shirt. It was clear nothing more was going to happen this evening. I'd sleep in the guest room as usual, no sense lying side by side all night and prolonging this pain. At least in the guest room I could masturbate and get some sleep.

"Look at me, Oliver," she said. "Stop getting dressed and look at me."

I finished buttoning my shirt and stepped toward her. I really did love her, I thought, even if she were weird sometimes. I wanted this to work. I really did.

"I'm afraid if you make love to me, I'll turn into a horrible monster," she said in complete seriousness. "I'm afraid if you make love to me, I'll kill you. I'll rip you to shreds."

I tried to speak but could say nothing. She was weirder than I thought. She needed help.

Forgive me. I shouldn't spread rumors. But it's not like Irena is my friend. I wouldn't tell on a friend. And simply everyone's talking about it. Brad doesn't usually kiss and tell. He's one of the few boys who doesn't brag about his sexual exploits. That's why I feel okay telling you this. Because if Brad said it, it must be true. Of course, I heard it from Nancy who heard it from Beth who heard it from her boyfriend Steve who says he heard it from the source himself but really heard it from John who swears he heard it from Brad last weekend when they were drinking behind the bleachers after the game.

She should have known better than to try for a popular boy like Brad. Personally, I don't know what he saw in her. He's way out of her league. After that episode in junior high, I never thought she'd have any friends much less a boyfriend. I guess you can't really call him her boyfriend. I mean they only went out that one time. And Brad's not even a starter on the football team. I think he might even be third string or something. So, I guess it's not like he's that popular.

Anyway, they'd won the game, really trounced them, so Brad and John were partying before the big party later at Beth's house. And according to Nancy, John didn't get it all straight, or at least that's what Steve said, so Steve said he probably embellished some things just to make a good story, cause everyone knew that Steve thought of himself as a young Stephen King. I mean his name was the same and all, except the spelling. So, again, I'm not one hundred percent clear on the veracity of everything I heard but I'm pretty sure the basics are true. I mean I'm pretty sure the emotions happened. I mean they were going out and all, so, I mean they liked each other. I know that much. So, I'm sure I'm not too far off if I just imagine the rest. I have a pretty good imagination. I mean I'm no Stephen King—or even Steven King—but I've been told I have a good imagination. Mrs. Barker told me that when she handed me back my freshman research paper on the holocaust. She said I barely had any facts in it at all and used real imagination. It's the only time a teacher ever complemented me. So, I'm pretty sure that I can imagine what happened. Here's how I imagine it played out—

Irena and Brad sat in the dark of Brad's basement, a blanket covering them as they huddled together watching *No Country for Old Men* because Brad was always going on about how it was his favorite movie. But I'll bet she blanched at that first scene where that creepy Chigurh character cuts that deputy's throat by strangling him with his handcuffs. All that blood on the floor. I'm sure she made him stop the video after that and put in the new *Pride and Prejudice*. Kiera Knightly is just so good in that. My mom tells me I'm just like her, which is cool because if I had to pick anyone to be like it would be her. Anyway, Brad would never get very far into *Pride and Prejudice*. That's guaranteed. I don't even have to imagine it. So, I can see them renting a third movie just in case. Something like *King Kong* because it has both romance and action. I mean what more can you want.

So, they're watching *King Kong*—of course I mean the 2005 remake. I mean, God, who could sit through the original. I mean I've seen clips from that film. The gorilla doesn't even look real. Anyway, I'm thinking that about the time the ship gets to Skull Island Brad makes his move. Of course, that was his ultimate goal when he suggested *King Kong* as a third possibility. It's got that long exposition. (Thank you. I learned that term in Ms Barker's English class.) So, he can wait until she's good and relaxed before he tries anything. And even better still, the movie is three hours, so there's still two hours to go once they get to it. Two hours before the parents start knocking on the basement door, or coming down unannounced asking if they need more popcorn or anything. It's brilliant. Which is maybe one of the reasons I like Brad. I've always been attracted to cerebral men. I know. I'm a pom pon girl. I'm supposed to date athletes. Not the football players. Leave those to the cheerleaders. Still, I'm going against type. But I've always liked guys who knew things. So maybe I'm a bit jealous that Irena got his attentions before me. Maybe. But don't worry. I won't let that jealousy cloud my story of what I imagine happened.

Irena's definitely a virgin. I mean the story goes that she's never had a boyfriend. So, she probably hadn't even kissed anyone yet. So, I'm sure Brad says something to her first. Probably right after Brody's shirtless character tells Ms Darrow just before she shuts the door on her cabin, "Ms Darrow, you don't have to be nervous." I mean, wow, what a moment! It's so romantic. He practically tells her he'll take care of her forever. That she never has to worry. She can tell him her fears. She can let her hair down. I mean every girl wants that, doesn't she? So, Brad knows this. And Brad stops the video right at that moment and turns to her, maybe slipping his arm around her as he does so, and he says with the same Brody voice, "Irena, you don't have to be nervous." So, it's just like they're in the movie. And he's Adrienne Brody, and she's Naomi Watts. And she doesn't have time to think as he leans in and kisses her, so she just does it. She presses her lips to his, and she's surprised by the sweetness of his breath. She opens her mouth, and everything is so warm and moist and beautiful, and pretty soon, they're mashed together, and he moves his hand up to her breast, and she moans just a little, just enough to give him encouragement, but not too much so that he thinks she's a slut, that she wants it, and then he moves his knee between her legs so he can rub his thigh against her privates, and she moans again, this time a little louder, but still not too loud because…well, you know why…and then he pulls back and looks into her eyes, yes, he looks deeply into her eyes, as if he's searching behind her eyes for her very soul, and he whispers to her, "I want you, I've always wanted you," and she pulls him closer and whispers as their lips press together again, "I want you, too," and that's where I get a little muddled in my imaginings because according to Nancy who heard it from Beth who heard it from Steven who heard it from John who got it direct from Brad, that's when she lifted up his shirt and clawed his back. Nancy swears that John saw the scratch marks himself. Long lines all up and down his back. And worse still, Nancy says that once Brad was really drunk he showed John the bite marks on his neck, too.

I don't know what he's talking about. It's not the way I imagine that night at all. I know she's a bit strange, but please. No girl does that. Not if they want to be respected, right? I know if I was with Brad we wouldn't have gone all the way. I'm not a slut. But we would have gone pretty far, just far enough so he wouldn't lose interest, far enough that he'd come back for more. And I know with me he would have been the perfect gentleman. He would have stopped when I said no. And even if I'd done something as crazy as bite him, which I wouldn't, though I would definitely give him a hickey or two. Even if I'd done something as crazy as bite him, I know he wouldn't have run off crazy like he did, or at least like John told Steve who told Beth who told Nancy who told me that he did.

Nancy told me he jumped up from the couch when she bit him, saying, "Who are you?" Nancy told me that Irena just sat there speechless for a moment, then started blowing on each wrist, over and over again. I don't understand that. Nancy says that Brad then told her they were through. He called her "some kind of monster," at least that's how it came down to me. He said now he couldn't even show his back in the football locker room. He asked her what would the guys think of him, letting some girl claw him up like that. She burst into tears. That part at least makes sense. He left her alone in his own basement. Nancy says she waited about half an hour before she came up. By then her tears had dried. She walked herself home. Brad had already gone to bed. Same with his parents.

She's lucky to be alive walking home like that. It was the same night one of the leopards escaped from the zoo. It killed a deer not too far from our neighborhood, dragged it into a tree. They never caught the leopard. Or at least I never heard they caught it. You know how those stories go. As soon as another story hits the news, we forget how close we all came to having a cat prowling among us.

Anyway, it's not how I choose to remember that night. I choose to think that after fooling around a bit, they settled into a cuddle under the blanket and watched the rest of the movie, finally drifting off together as the story finished itself. I've always been a positive person. I believe you create your world. The things that happen to you are the result of your own desires and wishes. So, why not imagine what you want. You're going to get it sooner or later.

# Dr. Louis Judd



Note: Today, I put patient into a deep state of hypnosis. She was highly susceptible, scoring an 11 out of 12 on the Harvard Scale. As is my practice, I used a candle, moving it back and forth before her as she counted backwards from one hundred. The following is a transcript of our conversation. I've left out the standard opening questions as they are simply meant to establish her hypnotic state.

"Irena, in our last conversation, you mentioned that you wanted to be liked. Has that changed? Do you feel liked now?

Patient's eyelids flutter before she answers. She opens her mouth as if to speak, but it's as if the words are being pulled from a deep well. "I have no peace for they are in me," she says. "How can I be liked when there are so many in me fighting to get out?" Both hands curl inward, clawlike. After a moment, she relaxes them again.

"Who is fighting in you, Irena? Who are "they" who give you no peace?"

Patient shakes her head back and forth, slowly at first, but then with such violence I almost end the proceedings before they've begun. Then, the shaking stops, and she continues, "There was a time when children played in the forest," she says. "A time when they prowled and leapt through the woods. Once the forest had the greenest of leaves. Once the forest felt the silence. Once I followed the silence."

"What do you mean, "The forest felt the silence? That you followed it. Can you be more specific?"

"The rich silence of being alone. Of the deer's sleep. The silence that holds the moment-to-moment foldings. I like the silence."

"And is it the children who are fighting inside you, the children who are in you?"

"Their blood-drips, too, are a language. A much older language. One I am frightened to hear. So, I fall between their words.

"What scares you about that language, their "blood-drips" as you say?"

Her breathing becomes agitated. She whimpers, almost like a dog. Again, I consider ending the proceeding. But as she speaks, she seems to calm. "If I open to their blood, I might lose myself. I might never come back."

"Isn't that a possibility in any relationship, Irena? I mean, if you think about it."

"He said my dress was cute. I wanted him to squeeze my

ass." She says it as a matter of fact and without hesitation.

"So, you and your husband don't speak the same language?"

"He said my dress was cute. I wanted him to say, "Fuck me the way you want. The way you dream it in your deepest sleep.""

"Why don't you simply tell him that?"

Again, she opens her mouth but no words sound. It's as if she is waiting for them from some other source. I almost ask her a different question, but then she answers. "No one alive says to the dead, "Become me." And yet they do."

"I don't understand. Are the children you mentioned in the forest dead? Are they who you are referring to?"

"I speak with their language, but I only know it feelingly myself. So, how can I speak it with my husband?"

Note: It's all beginning to make sense. Though she is American born, both parents were Serbian. She must be speaking of a cultural divide. Children of two cultures often complain of a divided self. They have two homes and therefore are of no home. That split identity carries over to relationships. How can you be whole in a relationship if you are not whole in yourself?

"Before our session ends, I want to return to your original statement. I will read it back to you: "I have no peace for they are in me." How can we move you toward peace, Irena? That is our goal, after all."

Patient appears agitated. Clenching her hands at first and shaking her head. Soon, she's kicking with her legs, flailing with her arms. I try to bring her out. "Irena, I'm going to count to ten. With each number you will feel more awake. At "three," you'll feel the energy flowing back into your limbs, at "five," you'll feel a warmth in your chest, at "eight" you'll feel your eyelids flutter as you move back into consciousness." I count as I stand above her. "Six. Seven. Eight." I reach toward her, ready to snap my fingers, but in a flash she grabs my hand with a force I hadn't expected.

"First nothing," she says, calm now, except for her vice grip on my wrist. "Then a swell of darkness. My hands so large inside it. Strong hands. Big hands. Ahead, I see the sheep, walking in the night like a blindness. I step, and they scatter. I crouch. I move slowly this time. My paws silent against the grass. The sheep like little clouds hover about me. I am among them."

She opens her eyes and immediately notices the tight grip she has on my wrist. "I'm so sorry doctor, she says, as she lets go. She has left a mark. She notices that, too, and turns away, repeating. "I'm so sorry. I don't know what came over me."

I sit beside her, take her hand in mine. "No need to

apologize, Irena. You have something in you that needs to be released. I understand these things." Our eyes meet for a moment. I must admit there's something about her that stirs things in a man. I've thought this to be the case before. There are certain women who through a multitude of unconscious signals let one know that they are ready to play the game. That they long to be longed for. I've often wondered if it's pheromone based or visual, or a combination of both. But with certain women, the effect is palpable. I steer clear by turning to Freud. "Have you heard of one of Freud's most famous patients, Sergei Pankejeff, the Wolf Man?"

"No," she says, attempting to pull her hand away, but I hold it firm. "He had a recurring dream of six or seven white wolves sitting in a tree outside his bedroom window. Their eyes fixed on him."

"Really?" she says, "I see cats. Cats sitting in a tree in the desert."

I have her attention. "Freud interpreted the dream in terms of repressed sexual trauma, as Freud tended to do. He suggested the Wolf Man had accidentally witnessed his parents making love when he was too young to understand, and it traumatized him."

"No," she says. "That's not it at all."

I raise an eyebrow. I'd not yet seen her defiant. "What is it, then?"

"He is seeing his reflection," she says.

"Freud would argue the reflection he sees is a metaphor for the trauma he witnessed outside him."

"No," she says again. "The tree is inside him. The wolves inside him. He sees who he really is."

"And what are you, Irena?" I ask, leaning in close. "Are you going to open to me? Let me see what you are?"

She pulls her hand from me and stands, taking steps toward the door. "I fear I must be going," she says.

"That is precisely your problem, Irena," I reply. "Fear. You fear the voices inside you. You fear telling your husband exactly what you want, what you need. You fear that if you do, he will no longer love you."

"I . . . I don't know what you mean," she says. "My husband and I are always honest with each other. We tell each other everything."

"No one tells their partner everything, Irena. If we did, we wouldn't have any relationships at all. My advice to you, though, is to tell your husband what you want from him. Find the language he understands."

She pulls her purse tightly to her chest, nods her head quickly, and leaves. I'm concerned I have not gotten through to her . . . The hypnosis has done its job. I'm sure of that. We've tapped into something long buried inside of her, something of which she's deeply afraid. I'm just not convinced it has opened the round door within, the one that sits between the conscious and unconscious mind. My hope is that we've pried it open a crack, enough to let the unconscious seep through. The question is, what will she do when it does, when the thing she fears rises to the surface as it inevitably must?

You know the moment the opening title graphics appear on the 1982 version it's a B-movie. Well, not a B-movie exactly, but also not the "masterpiece" Siskel and Ebert claimed in their show, *At the Movies*. A claw slashes the screen. Then the words "Cat People" appear floating above the claw mark as reddish orange sand blows across a reddish orange landscape, revealing skulls. Whether it's a masterpiece or schlock, you don't care. It promises something you can't yet name. But you hope to name it by the end of the film. The jungle music of David Bowie's soundtrack, all percussion and chanting. No words. You're entering a world beyond words. A world of desert people who drag a young woman—a virgin you presume—to the ancient, barren tree that rises tall out of a rocky landscape. They tie her to the tree and leave her as the color palette changes from red to blue. That's when the panther approaches, all snarls and growls, padding his way over the sand and rock until he stands face to face with the girl. He rises on his hind legs, wrapping his forelegs around her as if in an embrace, bringing his whiskered face to hers. In the next scene, the women of the village lead the young girl, who now waddles with a swollen belly, into a hut occupied by another big cat where she will presumably wait until she gives birth.

Something stirs in the far dark inside you. Not something you're familiar with, and certainly not something you're comfortable with. Like the original fairy tales, not the Disneyfied versions we see now, but the oldest forms we have, the fairy tales that were recorded by Perrault or Delarue among others, fairy tales that were told in the shadows from the firelight to children for century upon century, not to warn them of the dangers that lie in wait if they step off the known path and into the woods, though that was certainly part of it, but rather to remind them that the real danger, the only true danger lay deep in the forest within themselves. Within a half a page, Delarue's Little Red is eating the body and drinking the blood of her dead grandmother, only to be called a "slut" by the housecat as she gets naked and slips into bed with granny—the wolf.

"O granny, how hairy you are!" With each new exclamation from Little Red, we walk deeper into that forest. The place we fear to go. With each new cry, "O granny, what big shoulders you have!" we confront another taboo. Before Little Red ever hopped into bed with her wolf/grandmother, she committed cannibalism, and now with each "O granny," we move closer to what? To incest. Bestiality. Rape of a minor. The list goes on. And yet, we can't stop reading. And yet, here you are, age eighteen, sitting in the theatre in Buckingham Square Mall in Aurora, Colorado, and you can't stop watching as the *Cat People* moves just as quickly as Delarue or Perrault into the forbidden, the place you want to go, but don't dare.

And that's when you see it, crouching in the shadows at the edge of your vision. The thing. The monster. "I saw a monster," you tell your friend Rob, who came to the theatre with you. "I saw it, crouched at the end of the aisle." But when you look again, it's gone. And then you question whether you said, "I saw a monster" or "I am a monster." You turn to your friend, but he's so engrossed in the film, you realize he couldn't have heard you. Did you even say it aloud? "I saw a monster." "I am a monster." Is there a difference?

On screen, Irena stands in her nightgown over a sleeping Oliver at his bayou cabin. She watches, wanting him. Her hands move slowly, one over her breasts, the other between her legs, rubbing herself through her nightgown. An animal cries from deep in the bayou. She turns off the light and walks outside into the darkness. She walks slowly, painfully slow in fact, as if with each step she is discovering something new about herself. No words are spoken. The only sound for the three minutes and thirteen seconds of the longest scene in the movie is the occasional cry of a bird or animal.

She pulls her nightgown over her head, revealing Kinski's sleek, young body. She was twenty at the time. Only two years older than you now. She walks naked through the woods for the next three minutes. The camera hides nothing. Her almost boyish body with its seeming pre-teen breasts. Kinski owns the moment. There isn't a hint of the girlish shyness of her previous scenes. She walks with the same boldness with which she posed the year before for the controversial *Vogue* cover, naked except for the python wrapped seductively about her.

She hears another noise to her right. You hear a noise to your right. She stops and turns with the slow predatory movements of an animal, a cat. You stop and turn. There it is, again. We see what she sees, indentations in the grass. Tracks? We see what you see. A snake slithering over a branch. Her eyes now glow. Your eyes glow with the animal power rising within. She spots a rabbit. You see an owl takes flight. Now she's down on all fours, closing in on the kill. Your friend, Rob, finds you in the aisle, crouched on all fours. "What are you doing?" he says. "I saw a monster," is what you try to say, but all that comes out is a growl.

Kinski returns to the cabin. Your friend takes you by the arm and leads you to the lobby. Oliver wakes and turns on the light. The lobby lights blind you, and you cover your eyes. She screams at him, "Don't look at me!" Blood covering her face, her hands. She swats away the light. You make an excuse to your friend and run to the bathroom. You wash your hands in the sink, splash water over your face, and look in the mirror. "Don't look at me!" you shout. Who are you talking to? The face in the mirror, staring back at you, or the figure crouched in the corner, at the edge of your vision, the figure like the black arch of a doorway, a doorway that would take you where, exactly?

And you don't understand a thing. You have no idea why the scene plays over and over in your mind on the way home. You're embarrassed by the desire the scene stirs in you. Of course, you're no stranger to the naked, female body. You stole your uncle's Playboys a few years before and keep them stashed beneath your bed. You can't count the times you've stared at those pictures and given into your desire. But this is something wholly different. Not lust. At least not completely, though that's probably a part of it. It's complicated. And it makes you uncomfortable. Very uncomfortable.

At home, you feel nauseous. You tell Rob you want to rest. It's the same feeling you had a few months before when you were making out with your girlfriend and kissed her naked breasts for the first time. You lie down in your bed. Close your eyes, but you can't help feeling as if you're being stalked, as if the thing you saw in the theatre is here, now, in the bedroom with you. What did you feel, then? Desire? Shame? Desire mixed with shame? The harder you think the more it eludes you, the more you think about the figure you are now convinced is crouched in the corner of your room just behind the open closet door. That figure that grows larger and larger, stirring in the far dark as the feeling makes its way to your throat. Feelings and thoughts that don't reconcile with the guy who's second girlfriend left him because she wanted sex, and he couldn't take the hint. You open your eyes, rise from the bed and look behind that door. Nothing there. *I saw a monster. I am a monster.*

In the kitchen, you make yourself a bowl of cereal, unable to escape the feeling of being watched. You play the bayou scene over again in your mind, this time from outside your body. You see your gaze focused, cat-like on the screen. But there's something more. You couldn't name it at the time, can barely understand it now. You also see your body twitch, the way you squirm in your theatre seat as if trying to escape. Simultaneously predator and prey. Even while you hunted Nastassja Kinski with your newly found gaze, she hunted you. Or rather, her naked body, as used by the director, the studio execs, by everyone involved in the movie, preyed on you. There was shame around that, too. The blatant ease with which they captured your gaze, cashed in on it, commodified it. Yet another way you and Nastassja Kinski were the same. But did she feel the shame you did? It didn't seem likely, the way she moved so confident in her naked body through that bayou. Was she really in control or was that seeming confidence merely a cover (like your white shirt), hiding the long history of predation from her father, her first director, the entire film industry.

The TV looms behind you in the living room. Not yet the big screens of today, but big enough. A gaping, black hole. You remember all those afternoons after school, going straight to that living room lazy-boy and watching show after show: *I Dream of Jeannie, Gilligan's Island, Bewitched, Charlie's Angels...* You loved them all. You couldn't stop watching, unaware of the feelings Ginger, Mary Ann, Jeannie, Jill, and Samantha stirred in you. The TV watches you now, too. You're sure of it. Watching and waiting. But you won't give in. You won't. Until you will. Eat the cereal. Keep eating. Stuff yourself full. Stuff your mouth full. Stuff it so full you can't scream.

Of course, the bayou scene wasn't the only one that haunted you. That night you lie in bed thinking of the ending of the film when Irena begs Oliver to make love to her. He does so, but first he ties her to the bed, her arms and legs spread-eagled toward each bed post. You think about it, and again that thing forms in the dark corner of your room. Even now you can't write about the scene without feeling as if you're losing whatever it is that makes you you—or perhaps finding it. Like a map laid before you. Or perhaps a map you've yet to write, one that is more a record than a map, a record of what it means to wander into your own woods and get lost. A record of what it means to be lost. Or a map that leads toward madness. Perhaps they are the same thing.

Is this story that map? A question you ask yourself over and over as you write this. Is this story the path through the woods? And if so, where does the path lead? Does it lead to grandmother's house? To the witch lying in wait? Is there a darker monster at the center, one with whom you are, perhaps, more than a little familiar? Or is this all a lie? The answer is impossible to know. But you want to know. But you can't know. But you want to know. But you can't.

Of all the things that disturb me most, it's the fact that someone is writing about a woman with my own name, who may or may not be me. Someone is recording events of a life I'm not sure is mine, and worst of all, they're not giving me a voice. It's as if someone's watching me all the time, writing down everything I say and do, but it's not me. It's someone imitating me. It's someone trying to talk through me, or maybe I'm talking through them. It all gets so confusing. I sometimes get the feeling that someone is tying me up, spreading my arms, my legs, and tying me to a bed. It's very difficult to put together a whole. Why do writers try? I mean, what is a whole Irena? Is she an old woman in a black sequined hat and fur stole? Sometimes I think that's her. Is she something else? A young woman made of drought, for example. Yes, I know. A metaphor. But she can be a metaphor, too. It's so difficult to speak truth. I mean language is nothing if not a kind of apology, I don't know what else to say. An apology for being. An apology for longing. For existence. This is the way the world works. There's someone else in my body. Something else. Something talking through me. Or through him. Or maybe I'm in his body. I'm talking through him. Maybe he and I are the same.

Maybe we need a language to speak this thing out. It's like I'm giving birth. Only our child is a monster. At least he thinks it's a monster. Maybe I'm the monster. Maybe Irena is the monster. Yes, she. Let's keep her at arm's length. If she is the monster, what then is inside of her?

A dense forest where it's about to rain?

A forest with a river where she can put her hand through her own face in the river?

A forest with brackish water and gold-eyed animals.

A forest where she does just what she swears she would never do.

A forest where she takes off her clothes like so many sentences and sits quietly on her hands.

A room. A room is inside of her. An immense room filled with loneliness. The rest is simply fragments he invented.

Oh, but there's more, so much more. If only we could name it.

S cene One: Location—Cabin in a Bayou outside New Orleans

I step onto the set in my white negligee, and all the tiny tombs inside me open. The lights hurt my eyes. So many for a scene that take place at night. And too many people. They don't need this many people for such an intimate scene. I don't know why I feel this way. This is my ninth movie. I bared my breasts in my first at age thirteen. The number of crew members now is the same as any other movie. But now I have met Simone. Now things are different. Or are they? I'm once again going to be naked on a film set. This time, age twenty-one.

I chat for a moment with John who is already in his underwear. Nothing special. I just want to hear if he saw Margot again last night, or if it really is over between them. Then the director calls for quiet on the set, and John slips into his bed, and I slip into mine in the next room. The lights dim.

I wake suddenly as if called to myself by something outside. I pull the covers back and rise, keeping my focus on the window that never appears in the scene. The window just beyond the camera's eye. I turn and walk slowly as the cameras roll. I walk as if possessed. I am possessed but by what god I know not. I hope it is one that will cleanse me, but I fear it is one that will break me.

I stand before John's bed, watching him as he sleeps, my hands moving over my body, my breasts, sliding downward, pushing the thin negligee between my legs. I study John's naked chest, his leg protruding from the sheets. Then the cry that calls me to the unnamed god, the one I'm searching for. I turn. I stare into the void as if vision is a light that crosses worlds or leads to madness. I cross to the door, but the light of an oil lamp sears my eyes. I turn it off. An improvised move that the director will tell me later was brilliant. But I didn't think about it. I simply no longer wanted to see. Or rather, I no longer wanted to see as the person I was. It's time to find a new self.

Scene Two: The walk

I count thirty-two crew members as I wait for them to get the lighting right for my moonlight walk through the Bayou. Thirty-two pairs of eyes fixed on me. Of course, that's nothing compared to the millions of eyes that will be gazing on me in theatres around the world. But to think of that now means to lose myself, to lose my chance at becoming what I sense is waiting for me out there in the forest, waiting for me on the other side of this long walk.

The director calls for quiet. I have not experienced a silence like this on a set before. It slices through me, and I am almost undone. I am saved by the call for action. I know that place. I am protected in that place. I can be anything there. Go anywhere, and no one will know if it's really me. My thoughts detach from me, plunging toward nothingness.

I am walking in my thin negligee through the cattails, my mind becoming smoke, drifting into a thousand new selves. And then I'm lifting my negligee over my head, dropping it behind me like an old skin. One by one the tombs inside me open. One by one each chamber is licked clean by this thing birthing within. And with each step I walk I move further from the start of my own dreamed self, the self I thought I was. The self Simone prepared me to shed. Meine schwester.

The director shouts, "Cut!"

The world is so much noise. I keep walking.

For some reason, the cameras keep rolling.

"I said, Cut!" the director repeats. "Nastassja. You're walking too slow. This is not what we talked about. You should be bounding through the woods, a cat on the hunt."

Each atom begins again. Begins with each step. Each moment folds in on itself. We don't belong to ourselves. I know that now.

"Nastassja!" the director continues to yell. "Bob! Jim! Kent! Stop filming!"

Still the cameras keep rolling.

"Why is no one listening to me?" he yells. "I repeat. Why is no one listening to me?"

Why indeed. Why do they watch me in this most intimate of moments?

My father asked me one night, after he did what he wanted with me, if I still dreamt.

The answer was always no. Until now. Now I live in the dream. Now it is all I want to be. The loon cries, and I follow.

I used to tell myself stories to go to sleep. It was the only way. Stories of animals who could talk, animals who would tell me of a house deep in the woods, a house with a kind father and loving mother, a house they would lead me to if I was only willing to take that first step.

I step and step again.

"Nastassja!" the director shouts. "We are wasting film. We are wasting time. I expect you to be a professional. You are a cat, hunting. Let us see you, crouching, ready to spring."

Another voice, distant, as if from a dream. "Let it run, Paul. It's not what we discussed. It's better." Then the faint sound of an argument that fades like the moon behind the clouds. The cameras keep rolling. I no longer see them. I am free. Perhaps, in seeing me, they, too, have been freed.

I stop and face the camera, letting its gaze wash over my

body, as if it could fix it in place. A great horned owl takes flight behind me.

The director storms toward me now, holding the script in the air.

My father comes toward me now, holding his belt in the air.

I walk through the forest for hours, looking for a creek, a deer track, for any sign of the house in the dark of the woods. I spot the well first. Half-hidden in the shadows like a muted word. A muted world. Inside it is a darkness with no reflection. I reach into it, drink three handfuls, then open my eyes to a field of red.

The director's voice stabs at me.

I strike at him, tearing at his face with my claws.

He raises an arm to defend himself.

I strike again. And again.

He backs away, staring at me, as if he is no longer sure what he sees. Still the cameras roll.

I scent the blood on my hand and wipe it over my face, around my mouth. It tastes like my father's fist. So much is the same. So much is different.

"Give her more light," another voice shouts, perhaps Jim's. I no longer know anything for sure, at least not anything outside my own body. The light blinds. I wander lost into those first long fingers of light.

"Don't look at me!" I roar.

The cameras stop.

I see myself years later in another life, where I wake once again. My mind recovering into another unhinging. A purple garden in my mouth. Animals coming to eat the constellation of blossoms, forever blooming. Animals dining on this expanding universe that cannot feed us.

I remember. The last moment I felt no fear. The last moment I felt no joy.

I remember. Until that moment, I'd never bitten into anything.

I remember. I will touch myself to feel.

I remember. I do all this for you. So that one day I will do it for myself.

I remember. You saw me there. Are you tired of wanting me to be yours?

I didn't know if I loved or hated her. If I wanted to live the rest of my life with her or divorce her tomorrow. I'd been in relationships before, and it was never like this. Then again, I'd never married any of those other women. I must have married her for a reason. Right? So much about her felt right and good. She had such innocence, even fragility. Her fears reminded me of a child's, and I wanted to help her face those fears. Of course, she was beautiful. More beautiful than any of the others. I knew she loved me, cared deeply for me. But sometimes when I looked into her eyes, it was as if she wasn't there. Sometimes I felt like a part of her was always somewhere else, and that the other part longed to be there, too. Maybe that's what scared me the most. The thought that deep down she really didn't want to be with me. That deep down, she didn't want to be with anyone. She wanted to be alone.

I arranged for a three-day getaway in Santa Barbara. A little drive up the coast. A few nights sipping wine and retiring to our own little bungalow. I figured this was it. Things would work or they wouldn't, and either way I'd have my answer. If it didn't go well, we weren't meant to be. That's it. And dinner the first night went well.

"We used to tell each other stories to go to sleep," she said, halfway through our first glass of wine. They'd given us a window seat overlooking the ocean. A good sign. The food, too, was exquisite. I'd ordered the pasta. She had steak.

"What else were we going to do?" I said, the wine perhaps making me a bit too direct. "We needed a distraction from . . ."

"Oh, come now, Oliver. It was more than that." If she was angry with my comment, she didn't show it. She reached across the table, stroked my forearm. "I always loved the one you told about the fox who loses its way in the forest." She laughed the way a child might laugh. Like a light that could fill a home.

"*He meets a woman with moonlight slivering her eye who tells him . . .*" I began, though I didn't get far before she jumped in.

"*You are not the animal but the thought of the animal.*" She giggled. "That doesn't even make sense! But I ate it up. What else did she say?" Her eyes shone as if she would rather eat my words than her steak.

"Oh, I think it was some sort of nonsense like, "*You are not the word but the thought of the word.*" I laughed at my own strangeness.

"Oh, I love it, Oliver. You should have been a writer."

"What! And make no money!" I downed what was left of

my wine. I need to take care of you in the manner to which you've become accustomed." I'd meant it as a joke, but again, I'd missed the mark.

She cocked her head, unsure how to take it, then laughed it off. "What manner is that?" she asked. "Do you think I require a lavish lifestyle? Do you think I need all this?" She signaled our surroundings with a wave of her hand. "I only require good stories, and, of course, your adulation."

"Then you shall have your wish," I replied, taking her hand from my forearm, moving it to my thigh. *"Open your mouth," the moon-silvered woman said to the fox. "And speak your way home."*

She leaned in close, her lips parting. I used my fork to stab a piece of steak from her plate and fed it to her. It was as if her eyes caught fire.

What had lust done to us? I don't remember how we got back to our bungalow. Only that we almost didn't make it back. I almost took her in the car, then again at the door of our bungalow. We barely made it inside before our clothes came off in a storm of passion. Our naked bodies entwined, rolling about the room. We didn't concern ourselves with a bed. At one point, I pinned her to the wall, slipped my fingers inside her, as we kissed. Again, that deep growl I'd come to know. This time, it didn't scare me. My passion was too intense.

Her breathing grew erratic, which I took as a sign that things were working. I kissed her neck, her breasts. Her growl became a sort of moan that rose from somewhere within her body. She arched her back and stretched her limbs. The sound was almost like what I'd heard from alley cats when they are in heat. And then she slapped me, hard. I stopped. Stunned. She hit me again, then backed away, as if afraid of what she'd done, or what she was about to do.

"Tie me up," she said, almost a whisper at first. "Tie me to the bed," she said again, this time louder. She moved behind the armchair, placing it between us. Her hand lingered on the side of the chair, fingernails clawing the upholstery.

"I don't understand," I said. "Why? Why did you hit me? Things were going so well. I mean, you seemed so into it. And . . ."

"Tie me up!" she said, this time more like a command. She circled me now. I'd never realized how taut the muscles of her body were. The word lithe came to mind, a word I'd always liked but never fully understood, until now. She moved slowly, with the intention of the hunter, her gaze focused only on me.

"But I don't have anything to bind you with," I replied. I wasn't sure I liked this. The room an attenuated nerve of crossed desires.

"Use your neckties," she said. "You brought one for each day and a couple spares."

"My ties?" I wanted to sit down. I needed a drink of water. "You want me to tie you up with paisley patterns?" I hoped the joke would lighten the mood, but it was as if she hadn't heard.

"Tie each of my arms and legs to a bedpost." She lay down on the bed. Arms and legs spread.

I did what she said. Grabbed my ties from the closet and did my best to make some sort of knot. "What's this about?" I asked. "Why can't we simply make love?"

"Tighter!" she answered.

I tried, but no matter what I did, it wasn't tight enough. She could break free.

"Tighter!" she screamed again.

"Can't we just have sex," I said again. "This is too much." I sat on the edge of the bed, staring at our pile of clothes on the floor. I couldn't bring myself to look at her. I couldn't bring myself to acknowledge I was still hard. Maybe harder than ever before.

She was panting now. Arching her back and flailing about the bed.

"Stop it!" I shouted. "You're tearing the sheets with your nails. They don't pay architects enough to replace Egyptian cotton." Again, trying to lighten the mood. Again, falling short. "Stop it!" I said with a force I didn't understand.

She seemed no longer in this world.

I grabbed her flailing arms and pinned her to the bed,

telling myself I needed to restrain her before she hurt herself. But something else was going on I couldn't admit.

"Nothing can hold me to its center," she said. It was as if the voice came from somewhere else. She had that far-away look in her eyes I'd come to know so well. As if she were no longer present, or no longer wanted to be present. I tried to call her back, but it was as if my mouth was locked.

"I have forgotten how I sound," she said. "Won't you sound me. Sound me to my depths."

I held her there….and for a moment, I thought I might take her, just like that, pinning her arms above her head. Without care for her. Without care for anything. But she kicked at me with her free leg. Then she kicked again. Hard enough I was sure she'd left a bruise. And as quickly as the fire rose, I quenched it.

I let go of her and backed away. Feeling as if I was punishing myself as much or more than I was punishing her. Yes. I wanted to suffer for my thoughts. To look back on this day and suffer for it.

She stopped flailing and laid lifeless on the bed, as if she'd left her body. I gathered my clothes and dressed, slowly, as if I wanted to prolong that suffering.

During that long, almost interminable time, she spoke only once, "Don't let me wake into a deeper void," she said, then broke into tears. When I left, she was blowing twice on each wrist in that way she does.

I walked out into the night to calm down. But the harder you try to bury something, the more likely it will find a way to the surface. I wanted to bury my love for Irena. I wanted to bury my desire. She was too much trouble. Who was she anyway? This woman who seemed like a child wanting to be cared for or told stories to one minute and then turned into something else the next. She slapped me, for Christ's sake. We were just getting hot and heavy, and she slapped me. Hard, too. Her nails had cut my face. A tell-tale trickle of dried blood colored my cheek. The memory of the slap. The discovery of the blood excited me, and I almost went back.

"No," I shouted. I just wanted to make love to my wife. That's all. I didn't need whatever else this was. I needed her to be the girl I'd met in the Lincoln Park zoo all those months ago, or at least the girl I thought I'd met. The story of love is a fiction upon a fiction. If we tell ourselves enough stories, maybe we'll get along. Maybe we'll have a relationship. Maybe that relationship will last more than a day or two, a week, a month, a year. Maybe we'll even have children. The fact that I knew the story was a lie even as I told it, didn't matter. And that frightened me. It frightened me more than tying her up.

# ALICE

I almost hang up, the phone rings so long. I think maybe I have the wrong number. But then I double-check. It's the one Oliver gave me. She seems out of breath when she picks up.

"Irena?" I say. "It's me, Alice."

She says nothing, still breathing hard.

"Alice Moore, your friend from childhood."

"Alice Moore?" she hesitates, as if searching her memory. I have to admit, I'm a little insulted.

"Listen, Irena," I continue. "I know we were never the best of friends. Maybe you wouldn't even call us friends at all. We never actually did anything together. But I knew who you were in school, and I think you knew me, and more importantly, I always tried to look out for you. I stuck up for you when people would talk."

Silence. "People talked about me?"

I've said too much. "No, not really," I tell her. "Well, maybe a little bit. And when they did, I told them where they could put it." A little white lie now and then doesn't hurt anyone.

"Thank you, I think." Her breathing settles then.

"Listen, Irena." I go on. "I work with your husband now.

Isn't it a small world. Here we are, you and I, two Chicagoans, and now we're both in L.A., and what's more, I work with Oliver."

"That's strange," she replies. "He's never mentioned you."

Her voice grows quiet, as if she's drawing into herself, and I want to draw her out. I need to. I need a friend. "It's not that strange," I say. "He probably simply forgot. I've only been in town a month. We were just talking last week over lunch, and he mentioned you. I told him I knew an Irena Dubrovna in Chicago as a kid, and he said you were from Chicago. Like I said, it's such a small world!"

"It sure is," she continues, her voice as distant as before. "Oliver tells me he works through lunch. I pack his lunch each day so he can stay at work."

"That's right, he does." I try to reassure her. "We were just working and talking. But listen, I called to invite you to coffee. Just you and me to talk about old times. I could use a friend in L.A. What do you say?" This whole conversation's been harder than I thought.

She doesn't respond right away. It feels almost as long as waiting for her to answer the phone. Then, just one word. "Sure."

One word, but I'll hang a new friendship on one word. Rome wasn't built in a day, and I had a feeling this relationship would prove more difficult.

It's one of those trendy L.A. coffee shops I'd always heard about. Red walls covered in abstract art. Even a couple of chandeliers. You don't see that in Chicago. We like our coffee shops the same way we like our coffee. Simple. Black. None of this Vegan Coconut Sea Salt Cold Brew stuff. Irena was already sitting with her coffee—a cappuccino—when I arrived.

"I remember you," she says as soon as I sit with my coffee. "You were the pom pon girl who made valedictorian."

Things are looking better already. "Getting good grades is a matter of knowing how to play the game. Learning what the teachers want," I tell her, then rest my hand on her shoulder. Just for a moment. I want her to feel we are already friends. "Isn't this crazy. The two of us from Glenbrook South living in Tinsel Town."

"I didn't want to move, but Oliver really wanted the job. It was such a good offer." She takes her cup in both hands as if nervous she might spill it.

"That's my story, too," I say. "I never thought you could tear me out of Chi town. But a girl's got to eat. And it's great money. I couldn't turn it down." I point to the art covering the walls, the chandeliers. "I mean look at this place. It oozes money."

"It's nice, but I don't know." She hesitates, wondering if

she can trust me. "Maybe it's waking to a blue sky every day. Maybe it's the lack of big trees, but I haven't been happy here," she confides, looking as if she regrets the offer of intimacy the moment she says it.

"Well, that's all about to change, dear," I tell her. "Now that I'm in town. Now that we're friends. It's all going to change."

She looks at me as if she's falling. "Is that what we are?"

"Oliver tells me you're an artist," I say, throwing her a line. Someone's got to save her from herself. It may as well be me. "I'd love to see your work. Maybe I'll be your manager, and we'll get your work on the walls here." Again, I reach out and touch her hand, this time give it a little squeeze.

She smiles, not sure yet if she can trust me, but wanting to, I can tell. "I haven't drawn or painted since coming to L.A.," she says. "I don't know why. I used to love drawing the cats at the Lincoln Park Zoo. But I've been afraid to go to the zoo here, and nothing else seems to inspire me."

"Well, that's all over now," I say, scooting my chair closer to hers, leaning toward her in that conspiratorial way. "I'm going to take you to all the sites in this town until we find some that inspire you. We'll get Oliver to come, too." I wink at her.

She pauses, as if she has to think about what to say next. "Does Oliver talk about me, beyond the art, I mean."

"Well, sure, he loves you," I tell her. "He can't stop talking about you." Not entirely true, but the poor girl seems to need a confidence boost, and Oliver is one thing we share.

"Really?" she replies, innocent as a lamb. "I mean, we had such a terrible fight the other day. I'm hesitant to say this, but things haven't been easy between us since we came out here." She finishes off her cappuccino in one gulp as if she needed every bit of that caffeine.

"I don't believe it," I tell her, though I do. I very much believe it. It's been obvious in the way Oliver alludes to his marriage whenever we have a moment together. The way he puts on that pained look that says *I didn't want things to be this way, and I don't know what to do about it.* But of course he knows what to do about it. He confides in the new young woman at work. The one he wants to be his "friend." "You make such a cute couple," I say. "Now that I've met you, I'm positively sure of it."

It's then she looks right at me as if she's lost. Lost deep in a forest of dead trees, a forest with a stone house and a moss floor at its center. One she knows is there but can't seem to find. I feel a little sorry for her in that moment. I reach for her hand again, a vine of sunlight, wrapping her wrist. "What's the problem, dear? Maybe I can help."

"It's just that," and here she pauses, tears welling in her eyes. "I don't know how to please him. Or maybe I do know, but I just can't. Or maybe, . . ."

"It's okay, dear," I tell her, holding her hand now. "I get it. It's the oldest problem there is. Men and women don't often speak the same language. I've seen a lot of marriages, and I've yet to see one where the man and woman speak the same language, a *lingua franca,* if you will. In some marriages, the woman has the dominant language, and the man must learn to speak hers if there's going to be any hope of a relationship. Of course, he loses himself in the process. I'm sure you know men like that. Men who are dominated by their shrewish wives. And then there's the marriages where the man speaks the dominant language, and the woman has to learn his language if they're going to have a chance at survival. They're the most common. It was my parents' relationship, and I'll bet it was yours. My mom gave up so much of her life in service to my dad."

"Yes, that explains my parent's relationship well," she says. "If my mother wouldn't have adapted to father's language, he would have left her."

"In my experience, the relationship where the couple finds a *lingua franca* doesn't exist. It's a fairy tale. An illusion we're taught to chase. If you want your marriage to survive, Irena, you need to forget your language and learn to speak Oliver's."

"I think I speak the language of the forest," Irena says, softly, as if to herself. "It's an ancient language. I don't know if I can give it up."

What a strange girl, I thought. It's not that I didn't know that. I mean I'd known her in junior high, and she was certainly strange then. But who talks like that? No wonder they were having problems. How would Oliver learn to speak that language? The guy's as simple as you can get. He wants a woman who will tell him how much they appreciate the little things he does, even the things we do for one another that go without saying. He wants to be seen as a great man even when he does small things. In my experience, most men are like that. But I don't say any of that to Irena. I don't tell her there's no hope. I don't tell her that they clearly exist on different planets.

"You don't have to give it up, honey," I tell her. "You just need to pretend that you've given it up, that the only language you know to speak is his. Don't you know that's how the world works?"

She looks at me as if from across a landscape of splintered seasons, where the old ways of shedding one skin and slipping into another kept her from seeing the possibility of keeping that skin but choosing to wear something sexy over it.

# Dr. Louis Judd



Note: I believe we made a breakthrough today. Irena is becoming more self-aware. The low insight she exhibited in our first session has dissipated greatly.

"Each night I dream I walk in a forest, barefoot on the mossy ground. Do you see what I'm getting at doctor?" Irena sat upright, looking me directly in the eye. Something she was unable to do in our earlier sessions.

"I'm afraid I don't," I replied. "You'll have to spell it out for me."

"There's a cat inside me," she said, then paused, took a deep breath as if gathering her strength. "I know this sounds crazy, but I am a cat. A cat person."

This was a surprising development. Still, I've found that any time a patient talks directly about their problem, no matter how strange the language, it means recovery lies somewhere on the horizon. "Irena, aside from the slant of your eyes, I don't see anything catlike about you. What evidence do you have that you are a "cat person" as you say?"

"When I'm aroused, when my husband arouses me, I

turn into a leopard, a panther." She stated it so sincerely, as a matter of fact, that I almost believed her. Thankfully, years of facing similar such delusions in my practice have made me a natural skeptic.

"Do you have evidence for this? Have you turned into a panther with your husband, or with other men?"

"The only man I've ever been with was my husband." She spoke too quickly, as if defensive. Clearly, she didn't like my comment. "We haven't yet consummated our marriage." And here she paused, breathing heavier, as if the recollection clearly caused her pain. "Whenever we try, I start to transform. It frightens my husband, and we stop." She broke off eye contact with me, choosing instead to fixate on something on the floor. I followed her gaze and saw a silverfish scuttling through a patch of sunlight on the hardwood. It was late in the year for them.

"So, let me see if I understand you, correctly." I stated things as rationally as possible, in the hope that she would see the cracks in the story she'd created of herself. "You fear you will turn into a panther if your husband arouses you. When you start to make love, you frighten your husband, and he no longer desires you. Is that correct?"

"Well, yes," she said. "It's not exactly like that, but yes. . ." She stood, frozen for a moment, then began to pace. In the first step she took, she squashed the silverfish. It appeared unconscious, and yet, the precision of movement was uncanny. I felt I was getting closer to the truth of her delusion.

"Do you see that this is magical thinking?"

"Magical thinking?" she repeated. "I'm not crazy doctor. It's not magic. It's real. It is my reality."

"But your reality is rooted in an obsessional fear that you will change, specifically, that you will become a panther if your husband arouses you. And yet you have not become a panther. You simply say that you "start to transform." Those are your words. And that this "transformation" scares off your husband. How do you "transform?" Specifically, what happens."

"I groan. I growl," she said with such force it surprised her. "I scratch him, and bite. I want to do things to him. Terrible things. . ."

Patient stopped, her chest heaving. She paced the circumference of the room as if looking for a way out. Then moved to the window, her back to me. She was hiding something. I was sure of it.

"So, you have yet to actually "transform?" In some ways her case was complex. In other ways relatively straightforward. She gave me the language I needed to pursue my lines of inquiry.

"My nails grow longer," she replied. "I think my teeth do, too."

"Your nails are not long at the moment."

"I keep them cut short," she said. "Very short." She examined them and seeing something awry with the index fingernail of her right hand, she began chewing on it.

"Don't you see how this is magical thinking. It's classic obsessive/compulsive behavior. You fear changing into something other. The obsession is that you'll become a panther if aroused, and the growls, scratching, and biting are simply the compulsions designed to drive your husband away so that you don't have to face the reality of your true fear."

"My true fear?" She turned to face me. "What is that?"

"Why don't you sit down here and tell me?" I gestured to the sofa on which she'd started our session.

"What do you fear when you are intimate with your husband, Irena? What are the "terrible things" you mentioned you want to do to him?" For a moment, I thought I'd pushed too hard. If I have a weakness as a psychiatrist, it is that. I'm often too direct. With some patients that directness pays handsomely. With others, it drives them further into themselves. I wasn't yet sure which kind of patient Irena was.

Irena blew twice on each wrist, then slowly walked back to the sofa and sat before answering. In fact, she took so long, I was sure I'd lost her and was already planning how to bring her back. "I want him to tie me up," she said at last. "To use me however he'd like. To debauch me. And maybe I would do the same to him."

She meant to shock me. I was sure of it. But I'm not easily shocked. "Do you want him to tie you up because you enjoy being "debauched" as you say, because you are masochistic at some level, or do you want him to tie you up because you are afraid of those "terrible things" you want to do to him?" Again, maybe too direct. But I felt certain the situation warranted it. With each moment, I felt certain she was ready.

"I don't know!" she screamed back at me. "I don't know!" She covered her face in her hands, as if she couldn't bear to be seen.

"But you do know," Irena." I went on. "It is there inside you." I moved next to her, put my arm around her. Held her as she wept. I recognize this is not standard practice. But following the standard model wouldn't work. Not with her. I needed to break down the usual distance, the usual barriers. I needed to establish that intimate connection if she were to trust me, to lay bare her soul.

"I told you that each night I walk the forest, barefoot," she said at last, so soft it was almost a whisper against my chest. "I can feel the mossy green beneath my feet. I pause to memorize the ballet of flies above a dead rabbit. I crouch to contemplate the frogs that sprout from the ground after rain. I spot a wild hog crossing through the underbrush before me. It senses me and freezes. I keep my movements soft until I'm upon it. And when I wake it is with fresh eyes. I watch the cars and traffic lights. I see the crowds of people pass on the street, and I wonder why we assume we are outside of nature, when we ourselves are wild things."

I turned her face to me. Held her chin as I took my own handkerchief to dab her eyes. "Do you see how you're distracting," I said. "The retelling of this dream. Do you see how it helps you avoid answering my question."

She looked at me then, her eyes more green than I thought possible. As if they became something else. Something wild. Something I couldn't possibly understand if I had a lifetime to look into them. She leaned in close, so that I could feel her hot breath on my lips. "Do you see, Dear Doctor, how I'm more awake in the dream than in reality. Do you see how the "magical thinking" you refer to is what goes on in my waking life? Do you see the strangeness of the very idea that we are rational beings. That we move in ordered lines through our neat and tidy lives. That we behave according to a will that is wholly our own?"

You're in your fifties now. You've been married. Divorced. Children. Married Again. You've cheated. You've been cheated on. You've experienced life. You've experienced years in which you didn't want to get out of bed. Nights in which you dreamed of death. In other words, you are a different person than the optimistic, idealistic eighteen-year-old who first watched the 1942 version of *Cat People*. The teen who understood nothing. So, when you watch it this time, it is as different to the film you saw as a teen as you are different from that long ago now alien self. You watch it again and again. This time, unable to look away.

The film is justly famous for its most innovative gesture— keeping the object of dread, the monster, hidden in the shadows. The famous set pieces that have been studied in film schools for generations are master classes in the horror of absence. Alice walking home one night through the city, stalked by Irena. We see and hear only their footsteps. First those of Alice, then Irena. Repeat again and again, until we realize Irena's footsteps have stopped. That's when we feel the scream rising in our throats, just as Alice breaks into a run. Same with the pool scene—one of the finest scenes in horror, and yet there is no bloodshed, no dismembered body. In fact, we never see the monster at all. Only Alice, the friend, who normally appears strong—like one of the guys—swimming alone in the middle of an indoor pool at night. She hears something and stops, treading water, looking about her. We see only the play of light and shadow on the wall. We hear only the echo of something. Is it a growl? She screams, and we scream with her.

The producers of the film were furious at the absence of a "monster." We never see Irena's transformation. We never see the cat until the penultimate scene where Irena attacks Dr. Judd. And then the only reason we get a brief shot of a real panther is because the producers insisted on it. It is also the only killing in the movie. A low body count for a horror film.

You realize now that the 1982 version is the polar opposite of this study in absence. The Paul Schrader film is blatant in its action, gratuitous in its gore. Everything is shown from Nastassja Kinski's nude body to *American Werewolf in London* like transformations in which we see sinew snap and bones break as the cat emerges from Malcom McDowell, who kills a lot of people, mostly prostitutes. A much higher body count. And of course, lots of body parts and blood.

There is no blood in the 1942 Tourneur version. Just as there is no sex. Interestingly, though in many ways Oliver and Irena seem stuck in traditional gender stereotypes, the sexism in the film seems simple and direct, and therefore less corrosive than in the 1982 version. Sure, in Tourneur's film, Oliver occasionally treats Irena like a child. He is the rational male to her emotional, impulsive female. But in the end, we don't care for Oliver. All our sympathy lies with Irena. She is the tragic figure, and the compassionate one. We see Oliver as the fool in his naïve clinging to rationalism and traditional ideals. Irena is strong because she openly fights with her shadow. She is honest with herself in a way that Oliver seems incapable of. Further, she battles the unstated sexual mores of the time. And Alice, the good girl, the one who never lets anything get her down, the one who seems to know exactly how to get along in the world of men, how to insinuate herself into that world as well as into the relationship between Oliver and Irena, Alice is the real predator.

In contrast, the '82 Schrader film seems to support a conclusion you've been drawing for some time, films and pop culture imagery are not getting less sexist, but more so. Where Tourneur's film explores the complexity of intimate relationships, Schrader's film feels as if its only goal is to move toward the next sex scene. There is no nuance to the relationship between Irena and Oliver because they are never given a fully adult relationship to begin with. Instead, Schrader inexplicably adds a subplot involving Irena's brother, played by Malcolm McDowall, who is constantly trying to get his sister into bed. When, he's not doing that, he's seducing and killing prostitutes in true Jack the Ripper fashion. Women as objects to be murdered or fucked. Their nude bodies displayed as a means to advance plot. The Schrader film gives us women but not real women. It gives us death, too. But not real death. Only death as a means to spurt blood from a torn off arm or to paint a scene in the shocking red of a prostitute's gore. In other words, death as something to be feared or something that simulates fear.

However, what strikes you most about the '42 version is the way in which the film courts something much more terrifying, something much more unspeakable—the desire for death. That desire hangs over every frame. You know this desire well. In fact, with each passing year, the push for your own destruction haunts you more and more, in the same way it haunts Simone Simon's Irena. In America, we don't like to talk about death. Though we love to see it in our horror movies. We want to be titillated by it. We want to brush up against its simulacrum in the form of those mutilated bodies Schrader gives us. We want to get close, but not really. If we get too close. If we linger near it for too long, we might become friends with it. And that way madness lies. Tourneur's film is more honest—a horror film where actual death is absent but the desire for that death so present. Death and desire are never far from each other. The desire for death always walking beside the desire for another.

"I like the dark. It's friendly," Simone says early in the '42 film. She and Oliver have just met at the zoo, and Oliver has walked back to her apartment with her. Strangely, he stays for tea and falls asleep on her couch. He wakes in the dark, bewildered. That moment alone is stunning. As if he's waking to a new self, perhaps one outside the traditional American optimism and rationalism he seems to embody. When he wakes, Simone's Irena is humming to herself, a haunting French lullaby, as she stands in shadow by the window. "I like the dark. It's friendly," she says. A statement all the more disturbing because it comes from such an innocent, childlike face. Of course, Tourneur was also criticized early on for the casting of the French actress, Simone Simon. The producers wanted someone who looked more menacing, more like a predatory animal. But Tourneur knew the dissonance between her childlike face and the darkness inside her would only add to the horror. It's the same thing that plays out in our earliest fairy tales. The ways in which it is children who must navigate the darkness, for only children have the courage to walk straight into the witch's house. Only a young woman will open Bluebeard's door.

"I like the dark." You aren't prepared for the way Simone's line haunts you. The way in which it opens a door you'd rather not have open. There's a reason you never stop working. A reason you barely sleep. To stop. To have a moment to reflect. You don't like the images that rise from the surface of your own dark well the moment you are alone.

"And Levin, a happy father and husband, in perfect health, was several times so near suicide that he hid the rope that he might not be tempted to hang himself and was afraid to go out with his gun for fear of shooting himself."

But Levin did not shoot himself and did not hang himself; he went on living.

Like Tolstoy's Levin, you will go on living, but that doesn't mean the rope is not far away. Those images are getting more and more vivid, more and more detailed. And the relief you feel from those fantasy moments more and more palpable. Will you always be able to crawl out of them the way Hansel crawls out of the oven? And what about the writing of these lines? Are they a way down and through the darkness? Are they yet another attempt to bridge the gap between one human being and another, to reveal the darkness we share but never talk about? Or are they another distraction? Are they akin to Schrader's hotel room painted with the blood of the prostitute after Malcolm McDowall eviscerates her. The verdict is in. Guilty. Another distraction. But don't we all need them? Who wants to face the darkness of questioning who you are, who you are married to, and why your children have suffered so horribly and so long from the same OCD and depression that haunt you? Yes. You feel it, don't you. The guilt. Every day. When are you going to let go of it, Peter? When are you going to let go of the fact that your genes, maybe your parenting, too, fucked up your children? Your middle daughter has no memory of the worst years of her life. She's blocked them out. But you remember, don't you? And your son looks at you each day with eyes that tell you he's tired of facing his own darkness, eyes that ask when is it okay to give up? The sins of the parents visited on the children.

Simone's Irena lives in that darkness. She makes of it her home. "I love silence. I love loneliness," she says in the scene where she's set out a romantic dinner for Oliver. He comes home from work and tells her he's in love with his co-worker and friend, Alice. He says, he is leaving her. He says, "It's better this way." The male controlling the narrative. Forcing her to speak his language. She can't do anything. She is victim. Or is she? A contemporary movie would show her walking through the rain, crying, or perhaps alone in her apartment, eating ice cream and sobbing while she watches a romantic movie ala *Bridget Jones' Diary*. Instead, as in the best fairy tales, Simone's Irena confronts the witch, responding with, "I love silence. I love loneliness." On one level, it's a defense mechanism, sure. But on another, she refuses to run from the darkness. Rather, she embraces it, owning what we all fear. Silence. Loneliness. She begs Oliver to leave her in the same way Little Red hops into bed with the wolf. It is not the response we expect.

No one is wholly good or wholly bad in Tourneur's *Cat People*. No one behaves quite as we expect because no one can help being who they are; therefore, they are doomed not to know each other.

Oliver sums it up best when talking to Alice at work about his frustrations with his new wife. "In many ways we're strangers," he says, the frustrating impossibility of real connection, the despair that settles into so many couples over their inability to understand even the simplest things about each other, the wounding sexual grief from their thwarted intimacy, the realization we all come to face at some point that sex can only take us so far, that no matter how tightly we hold each other, how hard we press into each other, we are, each of us, alone. That's the sentiment implicit not just in this scene, but in every frame. Tourneur's film was never a horror movie in the way the producers wanted. It is, in fact, a story about the terrors of intimacy. The terror and, ultimately, the frustration inherent in attempting to know an other. In this way, it was far ahead of its time. How many contemporary movies dare to broach this subject? Fewer and fewer every year in our age of superhero action movies. Our age where a movie's success is counted by the number of explosions, the number of body parts.

The horror of Oliver turning away and lighting a cigarette as Irena expresses her anguish over their relationship. Oliver's utter inability to understand darker emotions, to understand anything that doesn't fit neatly into his naïve world view. Irena's inability to fit into his world of American optimism. His incapacity to feel her pain. Her inability to open to him sexually. The most painful and horrific scene in the entire film is not one of violence. There is no bloodshed, no ripping off of limbs. It takes place on the first night of their honeymoon, each of them retiring to separate bedrooms. Oliver knocking on the door to her room to say goodnight. He is dressed in suit and tie. The scene was originally filmed with him in his pajamas, but the censors were so horrified at the blatant depiction of failed intimacy and male sexual frustration that they made Tourneur re-shoot the scene with Oliver in a suit, perhaps hoping it would suggest that it's not the first night of their honeymoon but a mid-day business meeting, perhaps hoping that would somehow mitigate the anguish we see and feel on their faces.

Irena kneels on the ground on the other side of the door, her face and hands pressed against it. His pain is palpable as he says, "Goodnight, Irena." And it is as if we are the ones leaning against that door. As if we are the ones failing to connect. We remember the thousand times we opened to our lover only to find out they did not hear us or tried to fix us, or worse yet, looked upon us with hatred or disgust or boredom. We remember, too, the times we stopped ourselves from opening because we already foresaw the response. Whether that response was real or imagined didn't matter anymore. The effect was the same. Irena's despair, her anguish in that scene is ours as she responds in kind, "Goodnight, Oliver."

To watch Tourneur's *Cat People* as an adult is to confront your own sexuality, your own failed desires. Not those on the surface. Not the ones you show your partner, even the partner you've been married to for twenty-eight years. There are desires you can release and those you can't. Desires that may turn you into a monster. To study each scene of the film is to live in the absences, the shadows that you've pushed away, pushed deeper down into your psyche until they only reveal themselves in the darkest depths of your dreams. It is to recognize how alone we really are. To face the fact that the story of each of us cannot be fully told no matter how badly we want to tell it. That in the end all literature is a lie. A useful lie, perhaps. But a lie just the same. To sit with the film is to understand that the real horror is our utter inability to be known even by those we love.

Maybe that's why Tourneur's film ends with Irena's death, whereas Schrader's remake ends with Irena caged in the zoo with the other big cats, visited by her lover, Oliver, who first feeds her and then scratches her chin. Schrader's film ends with a closeup of the face of the panther/Irena, as David Bowie's theme song sounds in over the credits, *See those eyes so green.* Schrader's film ends with a type of connection and understanding, despite the bars between Irena and her lover. They have come to an agreement about their relationship. The film also gives a certain nobility and beauty to the character of Irena with the final closeup of the panther's face. No one has really faced their own darkness. They've just made it safe. Disneyfied our Little Red. Our Sleeping Beauty. There is no such compromise for Simone's Irena. Like Anubis, the Egyptian god of death, whose giant statue Irena stands beside in just one iconic scene in Tourneur's film, we understand, that our desire to be known, to be understood, is, in the end, destructive. Because we refuse to believe in the impossibility of that desire, because we refuse to embrace the silence, the loneliness, as the essential part of our human experience, our love kills whatever lies in its path.

Good night, Irena.

Good night, Oliver.

Good night, Dear Reader.

Good night. Good night. Good night.

# Irena

So much talk. And still no closer to me. I want to write a normal book, says Irena. I want to be a normal person. So why these cricket voices, clicking and snapping like twigs under her feet?

Better to write her in her own voice. Not his. That voice is laden with too many problems he won't face. Maybe a journal would help. Dear Irena, I'm so sorry you can't sleep. But it is a heavy burden you bear. You understand that don't you? The thousands of years of women passing their stories on to you. How can you be anything but invisible when you are buried by so many words, so many stories. In junior high you forgot to have a body. That's when it all began, wasn't it. When all you could do was sit and listen to the radio in an empty room. Every song another body wishing for release. Now it's the day that presses down on you. Now the day is your husband pressing down on you. And there's nothing you can do but write. Except words keep turning into another false trail of breadcrumbs. Why do you leave them, Irena? Why do you continue dropping them? As if there really were a way back home. You know you walk in the green and the black. You know the facts. You know that anything meaningful is done in secret. No one wants to see you become real. To become whole. You know touching cannot dissolve the boundary between objects. You know that a wife is an antiquated object. An object designed for a woman who no longer exists. And yet this object is lodged deep inside you. So deep you can't get it out. And yet, you are left hating yourself because you can't get it out. You don't dare let it be seen, do you? You know, too, the fear of letting one object inside another. How we desire it and fear it. And yet how kind we are to each other—mostly. How kind, until we're not. "I love you," he says. Your husband. Even as he grieves that very love. Even as he fears it. That's why you write, isn't it? That's why I write. Because so many words are lies. Because words and lies are all mixed up and maybe everything is a lie. Especially the words we try to write. Especially the words we say to each other. Maybe everything true exists in secret. I've said that before. We've said that in another story. Does that make it less true? That's the kicker. There's the rub. That you think you can contain the object by writing. That you think the more you say it the better chance it will be true. But how can a book be whole when Irena can never be whole. Maybe I should imagine that you are my only reader, Irena. That we are our only readers. You read me, and I'll read you. Is there any other way? There he goes, back in my story again. Or I'm back in his. We are each other's stories. Or maybe we should be done with this whole binary thing? Maybe that's the lie. That separation. Yes, maybe that separation is the lie.

# Nastassja

Feb. 25, 2005. I sit in a café alone, reading the *New York Times*.

Simone Simon, the French actress of near-feline beauty best known to American audiences for her haunting role in the 1942 RKO horror film *Cat People*, died on Tuesday in Paris. She was 93.

Words leave me. Each delicate hour passes through my doomed body. I read on.

In *Cat People* Ms. Simon played a Serbian-born wife who fears that when her passions are aroused she will turn into a panther that kills. Her casting in this film and its mostly unrelated sequel, *The Curse of the Cat People* (RKO, 1944), was probably inspired by her role as the devil's emissary in *All That Money Can Buy* (RKO, 1941), an adaptation of Stephen Vincent Benet's short story "The Devil and Daniel Webster," in which Ms. Simon's character steals a good man from his wife.

The facts of a lie. I mean a life. Maybe it's all a lie. A life reduced to a few paragraphs. Paragraph one, introduce a life, though they don't even give her birthdate. Perhaps that's because no one knows for sure when she was born. Strange, as they give a definite age at death. So, let's say her birth was in 1912. The next paragraph telling us why she was hired for her definitive role in *Cat People.* Does it matter why? How could the reason possibly matter? The implied reason, of course, being that she played a woman who "steals" a "good man from his wife." The language implies all the credentials she needed to play a woman so terrified of her own desire, or rather the manner in which her desire might manifest itself, that she would become a monster. Monsters, I mean women, "steal good men" from other "good women." Have done so for centuries.

…but despite her considerable acting talent and her distinctive looks, she failed to connect with a mass audience. The studio even tried to make her a singing star in "Love and Kisses" (1937) and "Josette" (1938), but she had a weak voice. Except for the four RKO films, her American work is largely forgotten.

In 1950 she returned to Europe to make films including "La Ronde" (1950) and "Le Modèle," one of the three de Maupassant stories in the anthology "Le Plaisir" (1952); both were directed by Max Ophüls. Her last appearance was in Michel Deville's "Femme en Bleu" (1973).

Death, you are the wax that seals what never got written about a life. Four short paragraphs are all she rates. No other details. Her loves. Her fears. Did she die alone? Yes. She was alone. She stopped making movies in 1952, which would have made her forty. I know that age well. I am forty-four. Forty. Just a number. The age when you suddenly become invisible to Hollywood if you are a woman. The age when the scripts stop showing up at your door. After forty, she had only a minor role in one film at age sixty. End of career. Is that why I could sit alone in this café in the center of Los Angeles wearing only sunglasses? There was a time when it would not have been possible.

No marriages. No children. Never staying with one man for long. What roles did she take on now that her career was over? No longer the "Sex kitten," the "femme-fatale." No longer the seductress. Never a mother. What role is left for a woman over forty if not a mother? A woman who the French Minister of Culture said upon her death, "We have lost one of the most seductive and most brilliant stars of the cinema of the first half of the twentieth century." How does one of the most "brilliant stars of the cinema" disappear? The answer, it seems, is slowly, day by day. Wrinkle by wrinkle. Gray hair by gray hair.

Her death drips into me until I'm no longer sure where I am. The only thing holding me together are the obituaries.

I search my laptop and find *The Guardian*, but it offers little more, except this closing paragraph:

"A few years ago, during the making of the Omnibus TV documentary on Jean Renoir, Simone Simon was asked for an interview. She refused, saying that she did not want to appear on camera as she was "a very old woman". Perhaps it was a wise decision, as she has left us with a vision of a lovely, young woman."

A wise decision, yes. Very good of them to confirm her decision not to show her "old" face was a wise one. We wouldn't want to subject the public to the face of an "old" woman. Better to leave them with that "vision" of a lovely, young thing. An image that can be commodified. Marketed. Sold. Projected on a two-story screen. It's what we want all women to be, isn't it? It's certainly what I was. I was one of the best at it. The reviews early in my career called me "the next Marilyn Monroe." They said I had that magic. I was underage for my first three films and nude in all of them. And the responses from the critics. Well, here's a typical example from *Time Magazine*. "Kinski is simply ravishing, genuinely sexy and high spirited without being aggressive about it." I was the perfect "woman" . . . . an underage child who was "sexy" and "ravishing" without being "aggressive." Oh, my voice yearns for yours, Simone. Meine Schwester.

Have I disappeared like you, Simone? Am I now to face the death of my former self? Can I escape the fantasies made for me? The scripts offered have certainly dried up. Even when I make the rare film, they no longer talk about me. I am no longer the child sex kitten. I am no longer the promise of what the male gaze really desires, or at least what Hollywood markets for their desire, the pre-pubescent girl. I have been married once, for eight years. Three children. Perhaps in them I have escaped your fate, Simone. A mother. The only acceptable role for a woman over forty. The alternatives— the Witch or the Invisible Woman. Funny, they've yet to write a book or make a movie titled that. When a man turns invisible, we get books and movies galore, even sequels, *The Invisible Man Returns!* I suppose a woman becoming invisible is far too common a thing. An everyday event, really.

And what if I were to push my way back into the spotlight? How would they see me? Am I then the Witch? Would I become a monster in their eyes? Would I be making the "wise" choice?

To be forgotten. To face old age and death alone. Is that what happened to you, Simone? Or did that loneliness, the unspoken desires of an "older" woman work deep inside you, churning and burning, roiling and boiling within until you became . . . what? A cat person? A woman of a certain age who chooses her own life? Who does what she wants?

Who cares nothing for what others say about her? Were you a monster until the end? The old woman who insists on being seen in public. The former "femme-fatale" who forces the world to see their wrinkled and decaying flesh. Is the Cat Woman any different from The Witch? So many of them haunt our past. Circe. Medusa. Lamia. The Sirens. Why are so many mythical monsters female? We are all of them. We are each of them.

Or did you slowly disappear? Did you retire to the shadows, curl up beneath the underbrush like a sick mouse? Did you always make the "wise" choice? Which was it, Simone? I choose to believe it was the former. That's why you came to me all those years ago. To let me in on your secret. To let me know that no matter what the press said or didn't say about you, you found your own way. You strayed from the path and into the forest. That's why the press talked so much of your affairs later in life. Yes, they wanted to make you into another kind of monster. The whore of Babylon. A Circe. Hester Prynne. Another type of witch. The woman of a certain age who still desires. Let the press have their fantasies.

And what will it be for me? With so many questions coursing through me from endlessness to endlessness, I exit the café into the cool, adulterated air. And then it hits me. Or maybe it was inside me all along. This air is my history,

I think. A forgotten breeze diffused into the world. I am no one today.

No one. There is freedom in being Nobody, like Odysseus with the Cyclops. Sometimes it is an advantage to be invisible. At least this is what I tell myself. I wander the streets. Let others see in me what they want to see. Ignore me if they want. There is power in that. I am a mirror of myself. Made by history's failure to see. And as I walk, I hear the footsteps of Simone behind me. She stalks me through the alleyways, and I welcome it. I give myself as prey. Let her devour me so that I may find my new language. I know "they" won't understand it. "They" will never understand it. "They" will continue to print their fantasies, to try and frame me with their stories. Try to make me their whore, their witch. The footsteps stop, but I am not afraid. I await my fate. Simone claws me. She tears at me, leaving me eviscerated in the shadows of a back alley. "They" can no longer frame what I have become—am becoming.

My new home is a language with no meaning. My new body makes what it wants of history's fragments. I rise and speak to the open air. *I come from the forest beside a turquoise river where the old gods float past, laughing and naked like children.* I will no longer wait inside my body with its hungers. I return to the magic of walking alone.

I had to admit she caught me off guard with the candlelight dinner set in our apartment. It had been a long day at work, a day in which I'd done a lot of thinking about us. Then I walked into our home and saw her standing there in that white dress with the red belt I picked out for her on our third date, her smile a lamp lighting one possible future. The shadows playing on the walls like following a ship into the dawn of another country. She stepped toward me, uncertain, clasping her hands before her, that smile buoyed by a hope I wasn't sure I could give her.

"What's happening to us, Irena," I said, taking both her hands in mine.

"I love you," she said, her smile fading now, as if those words cost her everything. "And you love me. I know it. I can feel it."

"I know, but people can love," I said. "And that love can tear them apart. It's tearing us apart, Irena. We live a life where time has stopped, and we're stuck in a sadness we can't shake." I sat in the chair at the table where the candles still burned, while Irena went to the kitchen. The candles' fire flickered until I wasn't sure if their flame burned inside me or me inside their flame. Irena returned with covered plates so the food wouldn't get cold, but I could smell the steak cooked and seasoned to perfection. She'd spent a lot of time on this dinner.

"We need to open to each other," she said, sitting now opposite me, taking my hands in her own. We sat like that for a long time, as if maybe sitting in silence, just looking at each other would be enough to rekindle things, as if all we needed was time. "We need to find that language we both share," she said at last. "A *lingua franca.*"

"I don't know what that is." Still the candles flickered, as if their flame was all I could see.

"It's there waiting for us," she went on more animated than usual. "We just need to look for it beneath the forest leaves. We can't find it on the main path. But it's out there. It's out there."

"I don't understand you, Irena," I said, standing, letting go of her hands. At last released from the flames. "Don't you see. You speak as if from a dream. But I live in the day-to-day world. At least, that's what Alice said."

"What do you mean *that's what Alice said?*" She grabbed her steak knife as if on instinct.

"Today at work," I started. The mantel clock we bought together after we were married ticked so loud in my head I could barely hear myself think. "I just happened to mention that I was worried about us, and we got to talking. She said you and I lived in two different worlds, and it made a lot of sense to me."

Irena stood and turned away, carrying the knife with her. She walked to the window, seemingly focused on a robin hopping from branch to branch. "She said that to you . . ."

I waited for her to say more, but she didn't. "It's not like that, Irena."

"Like what?"

"Like you're thinking," I said, walking to her now. "Alice is a friend. She just wants me to be happy."

"*You* to be happy?"

"I mean, she wants us to be happy." I put my hands on her shoulders. She stiffened beneath my touch. "We were just talking, and I think she made a good point." I slid my hands down her arms, took the knife from her hand.

She turned on me. "Yes, that we live in two different worlds," she said. Then she pushed me. It caught me off guard and I almost fell, dropping the knife.

"Irena, what the hell is going on with you?"

She pushed me again, but this time I was braced for it. I caught her hands in mine. "I'm breaking through into your world," she said. "I love you, and I'm going to do whatever it takes to break through."

"Irena, stop it!" I said.

"Look at your world now," she went on. "It's not quite the

rational place it was, is it? It doesn't "make a lot of sense," does it?" She tried to pull her hands free, but I held firm. So, she shouldered me instead, and we tumbled to the floor. Before I knew what was happening, she sat astride me, pinning my hands to the floor. "All I want is the continual remaking of the world," she said. "Until it resembles neither your world nor mine. Is that too much to ask?"

Or maybe she said something else. At that point, I didn't know what I was hearing, what she was doing. I felt as if with each ticking of that mantel clock I was becoming more and more lost. She stared into me with the green eyes of the rainforest. A wild place. She leaned toward me, parted her lips as if to kiss me. I could swear I saw fangs behind those lips. We kissed, and I fell into her world. We kissed, and I followed the river deeper into the forest. We kissed, and I became a stranger to myself, or maybe I became closer to myself than I'd ever been. She bit my lip, and the taste of blood broke the rich silence of my own loneliness.

I rolled on top of her. "Is this what you want?" I shouted. In answer, she thrust her pelvis against my leg, and growled. I pushed her legs apart, reached under her dress and ripped off her panties. Her panting grew louder, drowning out the ticking of the clock over the mantle.

"Yes, it's what I want," she said, her green eyes bigger now, as if the irises had filled in all the white.

I pulled her from the floor and dragged her to the dining room table. She was moaning wildly, as if she'd already entered that other world, and all I had to do was follow. I held her by the wrists with one hand, while I shoved aside her carefully set table with the other—glasses shattering, spilling their red wine upon the hardwood, plates and silverware scattering across the floor, the steak landing with a thud like a long dead corpse. I bent her over the table, pushed her face against it.

"Is this what you want?" I shouted again, though this time I couldn't fool myself. I knew who was in control.

"Do it!" she screamed, and I saw then her fingernails, long and sharp, more like claws, scratching the table. "Do it!" she screamed again.

Her bare buttocks shone in the light under the chandelier. The gravity pull of moons over a new world. A door opened in me, and I loosened my belt. Once. Twice. Three times I struck her. And with each strike, she moaned louder until the sound, to me, was like those of the big cats at the zoo I visited as a child. She scratched at the table beneath her again and again. It's only possible to be yourself when no one knows who you are.

I saw myself in the mirror over the china hutch, belt raised above my head. The feral look in my eyes. What happens when you see who you are? What you are? Does that "no one" include yourself? Was identity only a shadow game after all? The red welts on her skin stared back at me like angry eyes. I dropped the belt and stumbled backward.

Before I ran out, I saw her there writhing and moaning on the table, clawing away at it until her fingers bled, as if she were becoming some kind of animal. Before I ran out, I saw her turn one last time to look at me, the Irena I thought I knew lost somewhere in the dark depths of those green eyes. She looked at me, or perhaps through me. I don't know. And then she let slip a cry of anguish unlike any I have ever heard before. Or want to hear again. A cry like the mangled death of every world you've ever dreamed.

"Oh, you two again," the hostess says. "I've got your table ready." She leads us to our usual table. Oliver sits back to the window as always. I sit facing it. Oliver and I started coming here for lunches once a week, but soon it became two times a week, then three and four. I think our boss is getting suspicious. He hauled me in his office yesterday to tell me our late lunches were fine for Oliver, as he's on salary, but I'm still a probationary, hourly employee. I asked him if Oliver started as a "probationary, hourly employee," and that seemed to shut him up. But still, I better be careful. Make sure we're back on time.

"You look tired, Oliver," I say, casually placing my hand on his shoulder before we sit. "Is everything okay at home?" I leave my hand there a moment longer as our eyes meet, then I make sure I'm the first to look away. Let him know he has the power.

He's hesitant to speak at first. He pretends to study the menu, when both he and I know he always orders the same thing. Philly Cheese Steak. Still, I let him have the time he needs. Let him think he's capable of choosing differently. Once he's ordered, he opens up. "Funny you should ask," he says. "Things have been a little rough at home."

The invitation came sooner than I expected. "I don't want to pry, but anything you want to talk about?" I lean in, elbows on the table, left hand placed just so beneath my chin.

"It's Irena," he blurts out at last. "I'm worried about her. She's seeing a psychiatrist, but I don't think it's helping."

I reach out, gently squeeze his hand, let him feel the warmth of it before I pull my hand away. "I'm sorry to hear that," I say. "Anything I can do to help?"

"No. No," he says. "I don't know if there's anything anyone can do."

"Sounds serious." It's not that I feign concern. I am genuinely concerned. I just make sure I show the proper amount.

"It is," he replies, looking into my eyes, and that's when I know I've got him. I don't turn away this time. Instead, I hold him there just long enough to let him know I'm listening. That I've heard every word. That I feel every bit of his pain, though I know very well the only pain any of us are really capable of feeling is our own. "I'm not sure how much more of things I can take," he goes on. "I love her, or at least I thought I did. Now I'm not so sure. We're so different. I'm drawn to her. I know that much. I suppose that's why we got married. It's mysterious how much I'm drawn to her, but it's like she and I are strangers to each other, as if we exist in different worlds."

I can see the pain limning his mouth, the tears welling in the eyes, and I know neither of us wants that. If I let him cry in front of me, he'll feel ashamed. He'll draw further into himself. Men are funny like that. With women, crying together cements their bond. With men, it's the opposite. So, I wait for the food to arrive. Let him eat, get something in his stomach. Get himself together. And then I give him the choice I know he wants. Why else has he been cancelling appointments and joining me for lunch every day. The poor fool isn't even conscious of what's happening. "I love you, Oliver," I say, reaching across the table. This time taking his hand firmly in my own, letting him know, he won't have to work at things with me. I'll take care of them. "You know that, don't you?"

He seems startled at first. He almost pulls his hand away but doesn't. I know it's an act. Deep down, he knows what's been going on between us. "I . . . I . . ." he stammers. "I don't know what to say."

"Yes you do, Oliver," I lean in close, and it's then I notice Irena standing outside on the sidewalk, looking through the window at us. I wonder how long she's been there. Oh well. No matter. She's seen what she's seen. May as well play my full hand. "You know what love is. It's not some mysterious attraction. It's you and me together, letting the world go by. It's having no doubts." Then I release his hand and sit back in my chair. I've done what I needed to do. I've planted the seed. All that's left is a little bit of watering the fertile soil.

He takes a bite of his cheese steak, then wipes his mouth with his napkin. He misses a spot under his chin, but I don't tell him. It's kind of cute. And if I say anything, he'll feel awkward, less in control. If I don't say anything, he'll come around, and he'll think it was his idea.

Irena still stands outside the window, looking in. Her hands pulled up tight to her chest in that way she has. I pretend to look directly into Oliver's eyes as I deliver my last line, but I've got my gaze fixed on my true audience beyond the window. "You and I will never be strangers," is all I say, and it is enough. Oliver sits back in his chair, as if deep in thought. Irena turns and storms away.

## December 8th, 2016

Note: The following is from Dr. Judd's private journal. No copies could be found of an official transcript of this session.

Irena appeared quite agitated today. She often blew twice on each wrist, as if it were some sort of compulsion that would keep her from "transformation." She shifted positions on the couch constantly, occasionally standing to pace the room. "How could I have been such a fool?" she repeated after telling me about spotting her husband and friend, Alice, together at the diner.

"You don't know there's anything going on between them," I told her. "It could have been a business lunch. Simple as that."

"A woman knows," was all she said, then blew twice on each wrist once again.

"How do you know, Irena," I said. "Is this more magical thinking?" I gestured for her to return to the couch. She complied.

"I could see it in the way they leaned into each other, the way they gazed into each other's eyes. It's not hard to tell if a man loves a woman, Dr. Judd, or vice versa." She looked directly at me then. "It's been one of the few tools that have given women what power we've had over the centuries."

"Fair enough," I replied. "So, what do you want to do about it?"

"I can't say." She clenched her hands to her chest, held them tight.

"Can't say or dare not say?" I asked, leaning toward her.

"I want to kill her," she replied. "Maybe kill them both. I don't know." Her tone was flat, distant, almost as if her voice came from somewhere else, someone else.

"You don't really want to kill them, Irena," I replied. "Anger is a protective emotion. It keeps us safe from a much more dangerous emotion, grief. Grief hurts. Grief changes us in sometimes powerful ways, and that can be very frightening. You are grieving the loss of your husband, the loss of your marriage. Besides, if I thought you were serious, I'd have to report you. You know that. Therefore, if you were serious, you'd never tell me."

Irena didn't respond, at least not at first. She began rubbing her left hand with her right. But "rubbing" wasn't quite it. She had a firm grip on her left hand, almost as if she were attempting to twist it off. "No," she said, at last.

"No, you're not feeling grief, or no you don't really want to kill them?"

"No," she shouted this time, followed by what I can only describe as a growl. "I'm not going to let this define me. I'm not going to let them control me."

"I don't think anyone is going to control you, Irena," I said. Her oscillation between anger and capitulation presented me with a line of inquiry. I followed the hunch. "Have you heard of the Marquis de Sade?"

She looked at me as if I were crazy, or as if I'd mentioned the name of a forgotten demon. "Or course I have," she said. "He was a pervert. A madman. What does he have to do with me?"

"Almost nothing," I said, smiling. "And maybe everything. His reputation rests on four major works, two of them named after women: *Justine* and *Juliette*. In the works . . ."

"I don't appreciate this," she interrupted. She searched for her purse as if contemplating leaving our session early.

"Allow me to finish," I said with more force than usual. "Though the books are horrid, filled with all sorts of atrocities, there are lessons to be learned. Justine is passive. An object. A virgin, incapable of thinking for herself. She is a type, not a real human. And thus can only be acted upon. She is incapable of being anything but nice and is therefore abused."

"What does that have to do with me?" She started to stand, but I waved her down. She sat, her legs crossed.

"Justine's sister Juliette is the opposite. She flaunts society's rules in her hedonistic pursuit of pleasure. She uses sex as an instrument of terror, and in so doing becomes a terrorist, bringing the hypocritical and corrupt laws of eighteenth-century French culture down with her."

"I still don't understand."

"Don't you see?" I asked. "Justine is destroyed by her inability to step out of the role assigned to her of woman as passive receptacle, as object. She is punished by the very laws she believes are just. Juliette, on the other hand, subverts every one of those laws, legal and moral, and for a time, she thrives. But in the end, she desecrates everything, including herself. In the end, she doesn't have a self at all. You oscillate between the two, Irena. You cannot decide who you are. But you don't have to be either, do you hear me?"

"Doctor, I believe our time is up." She stood, attempting to leave. Again, I signaled that she sit. Again, she sat.

"Do you see how impossible it is for you to disobey me?" I asked. "How difficult it is to assert yourself? You are a twenty-first century Justine. And yet, in your heart of hearts, you fear you are also Juliette." I crossed to her then, sat beside her, and took her in my arms. I'm not afraid to admit it. The thought of being with her had tempted me before, the way her chest heaved, the almost feral look in her eyes. It was exhilarating, but that wasn't why I chose my next gambit. She needed a safe place to explore her emotions, the sexuality she feared. And I could give her that safe place in the controlled confines of my office, at least that's what I told myself. "Sade was incapable of seeing the truth," I went on. "He saw only two possibilities for a woman—either the object, the hole that asks to be filled, or the woman who becomes a man, the woman who violates others and treats others as an object."

She tried to pull away, but I held her tight. "The harder you try, the harder you will fail, Irena. The very passions you think will free you from the cage will in fact become the cage. But there is another way, Irena. Let me show it to you. Let me help you release those emotions before they kill you." It was then I took her head in my hands and kissed her.

She looked at me, shocked. For a moment, her face returned to that of a little girl. Only for a moment. "Doctor, I don't think this is appropriate." A little girl with a woman's sultry voice.

"On the contrary," I said. "It is exactly what is required." I took off my tie, my belt.

She stood, backed away. She made a strange sound, almost a whine that emanated from somewhere back in her throat. I can only liken it to that of a cat in heat, or perhaps a cat in a fight. I've never understood the behavior of cats.

"I'm going to tie you up, Irena." I said, standing, moving slowly toward her. "I'm going to tie you up and make love to you. Then you will see that you are not some cat person. You're not going to transform into a panther. Your magical thinking will be broken. It's therapy, Irena. It's simply another form of therapy." In one quick move, I caught her by the wrist and drew her to me. I kissed her again. This time, when I pulled away, something in her eyes seemed to change. She made that sound again. I have to admit, it turned me on, making it difficult for me to continue in a professional manner. I took the tie and wrapped it around her wrists, but just as I was tightening it, she broke free.

She lunged at me with a force I hadn't considered. I fell backwards onto the couch, and in an instant, she was on me, tying my hands together. I don't know if it was shock or fear that I didn't fight back. I prefer to think it was my own sense of professionalism. Let the patient act out her fantasy. It was the best medicine. Still, the strength with which she pinned me to the couch was surprising. Where did it come from?

Once she had my hands secured, she took the belt, looped it through the knot on my wrists, and then tied my hands to the desk that stood next to the couch. It was an awkward position, with my arms stretched over my head like that. And, I had to admit, a vulnerable one. For a moment, I doubted the wisdom of the method I had chosen. I saw claw marks on the armrest and the cushions of the sofa. She'd shredded it. How, I didn't understand. She straddled me, grinding against me, making that strange groaning of hers.

"Irena," I said, realizing my folly. "Perhaps we should call off this whole charade. I thought it might be a good idea to expose the fallacy of your magical thinking, but it seems you're taking this a bit too far."

In answer, she brought her lips to mine. Her kiss was fiery, passionate. I don't think I'd ever been kissed with such force of desire. A longing that had been pent up for a lifetime, if not longer, a longing stretching back through many lifetimes. She pulled away, just an inch, parted her lips, and I swear for an instant I saw fangs. But then she was smelling me, moving her nose over my face, then up and down my body. She was breathing faster now, more erratic. The scenting of me throwing her into some sort of ecstatic state. The combination of fear and desire was intoxicating. I admit it.

She ripped open my shirt, clawing my chest as she did so. Blood welled in the cuts.

"Irena," I shouted. "Enough! This is too much!" But she was lost in surfeit. Moaning still louder as she ground herself on me. Arching her back with a primal cry. Suddenly, I was afraid. I bucked and kicked at her, catching her with a knee and knocking her to the ground.

She landed on her feet in a squatting position, and for a moment, she looked ready to pounce, to attack me once again. Then she squeezed her eyes shut, brought her fists to her forehead, and pressed them there. Another animal cry escaped from her lips. She fell back on her hands and crawled crab-like to the shadowy corner of my office.

I hadn't realized dusk had settled. The scant light filtering through the blinds did strange things to the room. Curiously, I felt fortunate for the shadows. I did not want to see the war that clearly raged in the dark corner of my office. It was bad enough listening to it.

I'd never heard sounds like that before. Growls, yes. Growls and snarls. But not like the lions, tigers, or leopards in the zoo. Those were tame by comparison. These were stranger. Deeper. I tried to look, to see something of what kind of battle was raging, but what little I saw frightened me almost more than the sounds. Shadows like fists, flailing at each other. Shadows like the groans and shrieks of martyrs. Shadows shifting and moving like the darkest clouds. Shadows ripped in two. Shadows shredded and rendered to fingerless whorls even as they formed. Shadows spilling and spreading across my office.

And then as suddenly as it started, it stopped. The silence at first more terrifying than what had gone before. I lay there listening to my own breathing, the beating of my heart, wondering what would happen next. Would she pounce on me without warning? Had she already gone, leaving me here like this, scared yes, but also, dare I admit it, wanting more? I waited, and while I waited, I observed my own war within. What had I unleashed into the night? What had my own desire led me into? One thing I knew for certain, if and when we had another session, I would be prepared.

# PETER

**Irena:** Oh, look at you! Don't you look nice. A white button up shirt, complete with a red tie. You might want to add a red handkerchief sticking out of your dinner jacket. It's the best way to face your own darkness, the best way to enter the scene.

**Peter:** Thanks for your concern, but it's not like I haven't been here before. You've appeared in my work many times over the years. Just with different names. How dark can this really get?

**Irena:** Listen, if we're going to go any further, let's cut the crap. Let's stop pretending you're in charge. Let's stop with this bullshit of you as author. Have you ever really been author of anything in your whole life?

**Peter:** (clearly taken aback) That's not fair! But yeah, I see your point. Maybe fiction represents our lives more accurately than nonfiction.

**Irena:** Maybe you just write it to distract yourself from the hands reaching for you from the dark, the pale hands of an unripe bride. Do you see them reaching for your throat?

**Peter:** God you're morbid. Maybe fiction gets us closer to the emotional truth of who we are. Maybe that's why I write.

**Irena:** Maybe there's no difference at all between fiction and non-fiction. Maybe everything's a lie. Except dreams. You're often shocked at what your dreams reveal, aren't you? Things you'd long thought forgotten. Things you didn't dare remember. Perhaps the dream world is a much more accurate barometer of who we are, of what we're feeling. And fiction is nothing if not a dream. So many questions. So few answers. And yes, I am morbid.

**Peter:** Writing as another form of dreaming? I like it.

**Irena:** How many times in writing this novel have you been shocked so violently you've had to stop? How many times have you, I mean we, resorted to tricks to keep the monster at bay? Well, time's up. Time to end the games. Goodbye to binary of Peter/Irena. Goodbye to that particular monster. Time to bring out a new one.

**Peter:** What do you mean? You mean like the fact that Irena and I had sex?

**Irena:** Oh, you'd love to go there, wouldn't you? The old magician's trick. A little sleight of hand. Give the audience something flashy to look at, then hide the cards in your coat pocket. Sure. Sex works. Let's give them another trick, another evasion.

**Peter:** What if I was to say that Irena and I had sex in a dream?

**Irena:** Would you stop referring to me in the third person? Can we at least be honest about that?

**Peter:** What if I was to tell you it was the truest dream I've ever had? That though I had the dream years ago, I can't forget it. What if I was to tell you that in that dream I tied Irena to the bed face down and had my way with her?

**Irena:** Had your way with me? Oh, that's precious! That takes the cake! Don't you mean rape? Isn't that the word you want to use?

**Peter:** That's not what I meant. I mean, what I was trying to say was . . .

**Irena:** Don't beat around the bush. What else could you possibly mean?

**Peter:** But it's such a strong word. And that word implies intent. And . . .

**Irena:** What exactly did you intend when you tied me up in your dream, Peter? Did you want to have a tea party?

**Peter:** I don't know.

**Irena:** Come on. That's why you're writing this, isn't it? To get to the truth.

**Peter:** I never know what I'm writing until I'm done.

**Irena:** Oh, that's rich! You're really throwing everything but the kitchen sink in there now. Wait. No, I think you've thrown the kitchen sink in, too. Talk about playing games. What is this, two truths and a lie? What are we going to get next? The time you spanked your wife? That's fantastic!

**Peter:** This is no game, Irena. I did dream it.

**Irena:** I suppose you spanked me, too.

**Peter:** As a matter of fact, I did. It felt good. And you seemed to enjoy it.

**Irena:** You're not fooling me, Peter. I know you. All those nights as a teenager watching movies with your girlfriend down in the basement. Making out. Kissing each other, yes. But afraid to go further. Afraid to open. Afraid of where it might lead. Afraid of what you might do. She moans. She puts her hand on your inner thigh. Presses her chest against you. But you're a good boy, aren't you. And you have so much discipline. Despite the desire raging inside, you place your hand just beneath her breast, perhaps grazing it, but certainly not grabbing it. And you keep kissing until you both grow bored and finish the movie. A fine date. A really fine date. Good night.

**Peter:** So what? What does that have to do with anything?

**Irena:** You don't remember, do you? Probably repressed it. You don't remember the time you were watching that World War II movie. What were you, sixteen? Seventeen? You don't remember anything about the movie at all, not even that one scene where the Nazi officer ties his Jewish maid to the bed face down and rapes her. You don't remember getting hard as you watched it. You don't remember how you shoved a pillow between you and your girlfriend in case she might notice. How you couldn't kiss her anymore that night. How when you tried, you felt nauseous. How she asked you if everything was okay, and you couldn't speak. You don't remember how she lost interest in you after that. How she told you of her own dream one afternoon as you lay together cuddling in the grass. She told you that she dreamed of a boy who made love to her, roughly. A boy who took her despite her protests. And then she broke up with you.

**Peter:** This is sick, Irena. I don't know what you're talking about.

**Irena:** Stop trying to control things, Peter. You're not the author anymore. I was the one who had the dream. Not you. You couldn't possibly dream something like that. It's not in you. Or maybe it is, but you'd never let it out. Not even in a dream. Quit trying to pretend you're in control. You're not!

**Peter:** This is bullshit! I'm not going to let this continue. I'm done with you, Irena.

**Irena:** You don't have a choice. You've let the cat out of the bag…or rather the monster out of the boy. Do you remember that movie you took your class to in your second year as a PhD student at the University of Denver?

**Peter:** Yeah. Sure, I was teaching a course called *The Theory of Violence in America.* I've always been disturbed by the violence of this country. It's the kind of course you teach when you're young and idealistic.

**Irena:** You took the class to see Cronenberg's *History of Violence* at that theatre on Hampden. You piled the whole class in your family van and took them out for a night at the movies.

**Peter:** I told you I was young and idealistic. I wouldn't do that now. It was all serendipity. I hadn't known Cronenberg's movie would be coming out the same semester as my class. I wasn't even sure what it was about. I just took a chance.

**Irena:** You sure did. The class was probably eighty percent female, like most English classes. So, when you sat in the theatre you had a female student on each side of you.

**Peter:** I guess.

**Irena:** You guess? You either did or you didn't.

**Peter:** Okay, fine. I did.

**Irena:** So, now you remember? Good. Because when Viggo Mortenson's character grabs his wife and throws her down on the staircase as they're having a fight . . .

**Peter:** Yeah, Maria Bello played his wife. That was an intense scene. She was angry with him, and he with her.

**Irena:** It was more than that, and you know it. He throws her down and tries to take her on the stairs. She starts hitting him, hard. But it only seems to make him more determined. He forces her legs apart and grabs her by the throat, choking her.

**Peter:** This is not okay. I don't like where this is going.

**Irena:** Come on, Peter. It's then her face changes, isn't it. Right there on the stairs as he's choking her, pressing himself against her.

**Peter:** I don't know. I can't remember what I did yesterday, much less a movie from eighteen years ago.

**Irena:** Can't remember or won't remember. It seems like a pattern with you. You don't remember how she stops hitting him? How she takes his head in her hands and pulls him close, kissing him. What was that all about?

**Peter:** How am I supposed to know? Ask Cronenberg? Female rape fantasy? I mean, sure. Most of the women I've been with in my life have at some point or another confessed some form of rape fantasy. But they don't really mean it. It's all fucked up stuff. They don't want to be raped.

**Irena:** Of course not.

**Peter:** Any more than I would want to rape them. That's sick.

**Irena:** Of course it is.

**Peter:** And yet . . .

**Irena:** Say more.

**Peter:** No. I don't think so. I don't think I have anything more to say.

**Irena:** Say how you turned to look to the female students on each side of you to check if they were okay. Say how you saw the face of one of them, red with shame like your own, but also what?

**Peter:** I don't know.

**Irena:** Cat got your tongue?

**Peter:** Come on! We're complicated creatures. And who knows what I saw? I could have been wrong.

**Irena:** Could have been wrong? Really? You know better than that.

**Peter:** Okay, fine! Turned on . . . I guess.

**Irena:** Again, you guess?

**Peter:** This is ridiculous! Turned on. She was turned on.

**Irena:** Good boy.

**Peter:** But that doesn't prove anything. It's probably the result of growing up in a patriarchal, sexist and misogynist system. We incorporate that shit into ourselves. We can't escape it.

**Irena:** Maybe. Wouldn't it be nice to think so. It would certainly make things simpler. Perhaps, let us off the hook.

**Peter:** I think I've had enough of this. I really think we've gone a bit too far.

**Irena:** Oh, no. I'm just getting started. What if I said I wanted to hurt you, dear Peter? What if I said, I wanted to tie you up and force myself upon you, but this time not in a dream. Or maybe I'd invite the reader to use a strap-on and do me. If the relationship between writer and reader is based on anything, it's control. Manipulation. To hold you in thrall. To make a slave of you. To tie you up, so to speak. To shackle you and have my way with you. Isn't that what any writer worth his salt wants? Isn't it the deepest secret of any reader to let ourselves go completely, to find that book in which we utterly abandon ourselves to the other, in which we let that other do whatever they want with us, to take us places we never imagined, to make us feel things we never thought possible?

**Peter:** I wouldn't say that. At least, I would never say that so directly. Not ever. It would be obscene. As a writer, I don't really want to do that.

**Irena:** And yet you do. You very much do. Is there a more intimate relationship than that between reader and writer? And perhaps in that most intimate of relationships, if you were to fully give yourself over. . . Ah, but that way madness lies.

**Peter:** I'm telling you, I would never do that. It's not me.

**Irena:** Not you? What is this "you" of which you speak? Of which you're so certain? I've been inside you, don't forget. I know you better than you know yourself. What do you think relationships are if not manipulation? Pick one conversation with your wife. Just one where each of you isn't trying to get something.

**Peter:** Don't bring my wife into this! That's why I'm writing fiction, to steer clear of those waters.

**Irena:** But it's all here anyway, isn't it? A life laid bare. The emotional core of your life exposed.

**Peter:** No way! I've got too many filters for that. Too many walls. And fiction provides too many tricks to keep the truth just out of reach. Forget what I said earlier. Fiction has no special claim on truth. It's all lies. Every word a lie. I'm not following you anymore.

**Irena:** Oh, Peter. Aren't you the naïve one. Still believe you have control, do you?

**Peter:** Stop this! Stop this right now!

**Irena:** Relationships are just another illusion. Each trying to manipulate the other. To fuck the other. And then a baby is born…And that baby is the monster they've created together. I'm not talking about a real flesh and blood child. I'm talking about what happens when two people get together. A third thing is created. Something other. Something that comes from each of them but is different from them. A thing. A monster created to make us feel as if we aren't alone. But we are alone. Very much alone.

**Peter:** My marriage is real.

**Irena:** I'm sure it is. But it doesn't change the facts.

**Peter:** What facts?

**Irena:** That any relationship involves a third, invisible thing.

**Peter:** Sure, my relationship is not perfect. No relationship is, but that doesn't make it monstrous.

**Irena:** I'm not saying the relationship is monstrous. I'm saying what it creates, what it sets free is monstrous. Oh, but look at the way you tear each other down. How that thing grows between you, until neither of you can see the other.

**Peter:** That's not true! We help each other, too. We do!

**Irena:** Again, so certain. Me thinks he doth protest too much. If the evidence of life shows us anything it's that uncertainty lies at the center of everything. We don't know anything for sure until it's done. Until it's over. Until then, the potentiality is there. We exist in that potentiality. Except we pretend we don't. We repress. We dismiss. We never ever admit to the thoughts churning inside us. But does that make them any less real. Come on, Peter! Wake up! The history of the world, the history of relationships is the history of that potentiality.

**Peter:** It's all starting to make sense now. You've finally convinced me. You've convinced me that you're crazy! This is why Dr. Judd diagnosed you with OCD. It's a serious disorder, not the way it's portrayed on TV. In severe cases like yours it's often mistaken for Schizophrenia.

**Irena:** Don't try to turn the tables on me. I'm not done with you yet. Obsessive Compulsive Disorder is the intense fear of something generally involving an inability to accept uncertainty. That's you!

**Peter:** Don't lecture me on OCD! How dare you!

**Irena:** Most people think it's characterized by an obsession about germs which leads to compulsive behaviors designed to keep the person suffering from OCD from "catching" those germs. But that's not really it at all. It's only the form most understood by the public. The form most easily consumable by the media. It's all about uncertainty!

**Peter:** Bullshit! I know what you're trying to do, and I'm not going to let you do it. You can't pin this on me.

**Irena:** It's already on you. Has been all the time.

**Peter:** Really? Well let's see how you like it when the tables are turned. OCD can take on many forms that are just as common but not as well known. Maybe the obsession that the sufferer will change into something or someone they fear unless they perform certain compulsions.

**Irena:** Stop it! I don't want to hear this!

**Peter:** Someone who is intensely smart fears they will become dumb. A woman who is sexual fears she will become a monster.

**Irena:** You're not going to do this to me! What about the boy who is incredibly sweet, the one who goes out of his way to be understanding in all things with women, the one who fears he might become a misogynist or worse, a rapist. It's the perversion of the disease, the perversion of our minds to prey on the things we love. To turn them into things we fear or hate or make us think we are capable of fearing or hating.

**Peter:** I would argue it's the perversion of life that does that.

**Irena:** I wouldn't disagree.

**Peter:** My point is that it's not really the disease. It's not really the OCD. Our minds do it anyway. OCD just amplifies what's already there, what's already being repressed.

**Irena:** Your family has a long history with OCD, doesn't it? You know this disorder well. Maybe because you suffer from it.

**Peter:** No shit, Sherlock. You think that's a revelation?

**Irena:** Maybe you're that boy, and . . .

**Peter:** I'm saying we all suffer from it, and it's our fear of talking about it that keeps all the shit happening in the world.

**Irena:** Maybe you're simply trying to pin it on me. Wouldn't that be typical! The man pinning his sins on the woman. It's been going on for centuries, I guess, so why stop now. Make me the monster. Turn me into your Medusa! Well, I'll tell you what. We did have sex in your dream! And it was the best sex you've ever had. It was the closest you'll ever come to being an object inseparable from another object. You dissolved completely. There was no longer a world. Just us. You and me. The whole we long for. We had it. We were there. And I was the one in control. I was the one fucking you! And we were a whole. You and I a whole. And then I rolled off, and all I could think about was killing you. And you me. Because we were alone again. Alone with no body to shield us from ourselves.

End Scene

Who is this person left standing in the middle of these woods? I don't understand this person. I don't know him or her. How can we look inside an atom or outward to the universe when we can't even look inside ourselves? Not without lies and self-deception creeping in around every sentence, every paragraph. What is it Tolstoy said? "Art is a microscope which the artist fixes on the secrets of the soul and shows to people these secrets which are common to all." Well, I'm no Tolstoy. My microscope is fuzzy at best, the lens cracked. Or perhaps his lens was cracked, at least the lens that told him he could be so certain about those "secrets of the soul." Perhaps, it's all a lie. If so, what hope is there for Irena? For me? For us? Maybe Tolstoy said that just so he could keep going. I can't blame him. We all need our illusions. Maybe we never get closer to the truth. Maybe we just keep making more elaborate illusions.

And if dreaming is part of life, maybe writing is also a part of life. Writing as life. A life of sorts. A Frankenstein's monster of life. A monster made up of parts of who we are, parts of the people we know, with loneliness and unfulfilled desire churning at the core, working in the darkness, until they spark to life that thing we've kept locked away in a castle tower or in a house deep in the dark woods of our uncharted lives. Maybe that's the best we can hope for. Not truth. Never truth. But a Frankenstein's monster version of truth. A poorly made simulacra that makes us feel as if we've created something real. We fear the real monster and keep it inside. And that fact keeps us from letting others see, truly see, who we are, who we are capable of becoming. A cage within a cage within a cage. Only the monster comes back to destroy Dr. Frankenstein in the end. The creation always returns to seek vengeance on its creator.

Given the chaos of the previous chapter, maybe it's best if we take a more objective look. My Journal entries and possessions. I mean her journal entries and possessions. Things like that. Let's look at her. Irena. Us. Shall we? Unfortunately, we didn't date her entries. But she never did feel I existed in time anyway.

Saturday: I wanted to go out. I didn't care about the rain. I wanted to have a coffee. I wanted to sit at a window table and draw. But at the café, three girls sat beneath the awning in the rain. I changed my mind and turned down an alley, not sure where I would go. In the alley, I saw two, tall boarded-up windows. A secret life lives there.

Sunday: I met a man today. He approached me at the zoo while I was drawing. He came home with me after.

Wednesday: On the way home from work, I took the long way through the park. I spotted a fox. Red fur streaking through the dappled sunlight between the trees. What a stunning creature! The world made sense. I thought about running with her but decided against it. The man was waiting for me when I got home.

Saturday: The ant is close now. Close to the other. It is hungry. It caresses the other ants' mouth. The other regurgitates whatever food she is carrying into the other. It is beautiful and terribly, terribly sad. I think I need to be alone.

Monday: Every day I wake and think about creatures who need each other. They are all in the process of becoming, and I have only tenderness for that. Except on the days when I want to hit someone, to tear into them until there's nothing left.

Tuesday: Oliver brought me a cat, but I didn't like it. Or rather, it didn't like me. Then he bought me a bird. The bird didn't like me either. I don't know if Oliver likes me. He says he does, but what does that mean when he can't see me?

Thursday: I look at the things we call dead. Rocks. Furniture. TVs. People. I can't see into any of them. It's like they're objects. And yet, they somehow work their way inside me as if they want to eject me from myself. Eject me from the world. As if they want me, too, to be an object.

Sunday: I don't want to live in a world without fireflies. Oliver says we're to move to Los Angeles.

Monday: I'm no longer afraid of the dark. Sometimes I wander into Oliver's room and listen to him breathing. His breath is like no color I've seen in the world. But his breath is not him. I cannot see him. When I try, all I want to do is eat him. Tear him limb from limb and devour him.

Tuesday: The cicadas are restless today. I didn't know they had them here. I'm restless, too. I've been pinned to a board. And the board is Los Angeles. Except no one looks at anyone here.

Friday: The world is smaller than we think. Alice called me today. What must it be like to wear your own body? The body I wear feels like a punchline. Like thrashing grasses. Like hollow, thirsty eyes. She asks me if I can see Oliver. I tell her how can I crawl through a void, I mean claw through a void.

Saturday: The wind whistles through the dark holes in your hands. Through the dark holes in a face that doesn't belong to you anymore. I hear the hollow echoes of every creature that I've become. I have no sense of the present. The past is a dream where I want to remain.

Sunday: I spent the afternoon watching the death throes of a fly. It dies beneath the gooseneck lamp on my desk. Before he died, he touched everything—my papers, my pens, my notebook, even the dead skin cells and hair that fell from me. I know I'm the only person to have ever seen him. To have ever touched him. Will there be another to touch my dead cells, to take them inside? Will there be another to touch me?

Wednesday: It rarely rains here in L.A. My body exists in the rain. I exist in the window inside the rain.

Friday: There is a creature moving about inside me. I don't know what it is. I don't know if it's a monster. I only know Dr. Judd is wrong. I also know that what I hate is not the monster but the moment. The moment my husband returns, and, filled with longing, I go to him.

Sunday: Very little to write today. My husband is working. The monster is sleeping.

Tuesday: I need to kill the idea that everything will be okay when my husband comes home. I need to stop thinking my husband can see. I alone see. I see that it was all a lie. I see I must kill the creature inside to be a good wife. Irena alone.

Thursday: It's as though everything around me is part of this body.

The saltshaker. The candle. The throw pillow and blanket. The purse. Especially the purse. The cell phone. The bottle of lotion. The TV remote. The carpet. The end table. The floss. The headphones and books. The vitamins and spices. The rice maker. The clocks. So many clocks. Each one keeping a different time in a different part of my body. The mirrors, too. They are the worst because they are false.

As soon as I go out into the street, there's more I need to put in this body. So much more it is overwhelming. And then I don't know who I am. I don't understand people. Especially people who've never felt the deep horror of their own difference.

Who is Irena?

What is this creature inside?

Monday: Rage destroys me.

# Nastassja

I hadn't planned to meet her there. I had no reason to think she would be there at all. And yet, there she was, standing in front of the big cat cages, watching them pace back and forth. Something about her was different from when I saw her last. It had only been nine months, perhaps longer. But she'd changed. Her clothes for one thing. Darker colors with little skin showing. And she'd put her hair up. No longer the little girl. She held a sketch pad, and she was drawing furiously in it. A forest on every page.

"Is there a page for me, meine schwester?" I asked, touching her shoulder gently as I did so, letting her know I was a friend.

She jumped, dropping her drawing pencil. I picked it up, handed it back to her.

"I'm sorry," she said, staring at me. "Do I know you?"

"Not exactly," I replied, then lowered my sunglasses.

"You're the woman from the restaurant on my wedding night, aren't you?" She covered her drawing as if afraid I might want to see it.

"Yes, I am."

"More than that," she went on. "You're famous." She took a step back as if to take all of me in. "I didn't recognize you that night, what was it, nine months ago? But I thought about you after. I thought maybe you were that actress. Though I never saw any of your movies. I'm sorry."

"No need to apologize, Irena" I replied. "I don't make them very often anymore. And the old ones . . . well, if you're interested, I guess you can rent them."

"How do you know my name?" she asked, shifting back to fear. Muscles taut. Ready to pounce.

"We are sisters," I replied, spoken as a simple fact.

"But I have no sisters," she stepped further away, perhaps wondering if I were crazy.

"The woods are not as empty as you might think," I said, giving nothing away.

She needed to find the path of her own accord. Her knees buckled. I stepped quickly and caught her in my arms. Nothing quite like the terror of syntax. "Let me help you, dear," I went on, taking her arm in mine, leading her to a nearby bench. We sat silently together for quite some time. The December air was cool, but not cold. Upper 60's. In fact, it was quite pleasant. And then one of our kind passed by, The red-petaled dress and purposeful saunter giving her away. The choice to be loud in a world that preferred her muted.

"Did you mark that one?" I asked Irena. "Another sister."

"Really?" she said. "How do you know?"

"Watch. You'll see." Sure enough another emerged from a small crowd not two minutes later. The cadence of her walk dense, tropical.

Irena pointed. "Is she a sister, too?"

I lowered her hand. "Yes," I said. "But we don't need to be obvious." I took her again by the arm, pulled her to her feet. "Why don't we walk and talk?" We didn't speak for a long time, strolling past the pachyderms, watching as they huddled in a nervous herd.

"I don't understand," Irena said, breaking the silence. "What are you doing here? Why are you talking to me? Why do you call me sister? Why is that other woman my sister, too?"

"So many questions," I said. "I can't possibly answer them all." I stopped, pulling her to face me. "I didn't even expect to find you here. I only know I felt I had to be here, at the zoo, today."

"Me, too," she said, "Me, too. In fact, I haven't been to the zoo since moving to L.A."

"There's your first answer," I said, but she looked puzzled. "The world is not rational. We grow up in a system, a male system, that tells us the world is rational. Every day. And soon we believe it, too. We have to believe it. But that doesn't make it true. And it's not the only system in the world. There are other systems. Older ones. You and I here today, talking, is proof of that."

"Proof that we are sisters," she said, smiling conspiratorially at me.

"Yes." I winked. "Your story is not so rare or original, Irena."

"What do you mean?" she asked. Now pulling me closer to her. "I mean, I never thought I was original. I don't think I thought about it at all."

In answer, I took the sketchbook from her hand, flipped it open. She made no protest. "Look, Irena," I said. "You stood in front of cages with cats in isolation, but what you've drawn are cats together, lounging about an ancient tree."

"It's a recurring dream I have," she said. "A dream I don't understand."

I gave her back her sketchbook. "There's a long history of sisters who have lived your story," I replied. "Many of us who've lived through many seasons of destruction. I think one season is enough for you." Again, I must have hit a nerve. Tears welled in her eyes. She brought her hands tightly to her chest. I took them in my own. "They will be making their move soon," I said. "You need to decide yours."

"Who will be making their move?" She looked at me, as if confused, though I could see the light of understanding in her eyes, even as she finished her question.

"You know who," I replied. "Do not think you are stuck here, that you don't belong anywhere else."

At that moment, an extraordinarily tall woman passed by, a woman dressed in leaves, her many shades of green dazzling in the mid-afternoon sun. She slowed as she passed us, nodding in acknowledgement. "It's time to unstitch your story, Irena," I said. "Time to see what you want to see."

We walked the circumference of the zoo without saying another word. I could tell Irena was deep in thought. And truth be told, so was I. I hadn't expected to meet her again. Not here. And yet there she was. Surprising me, but of course not really surprising me. I still had many lessons to learn if I was to avoid Simone's fate, or the fate I feared may have been hers. When Irena and I parted that afternoon, she hugged me, holding me tightly to her, so tightly I thought she might never let go. I held her back just as tightly because it felt good. It felt like home. Not the home I was raised in. God, no. That home was a nightmare from which it took a lifetime to wake. But the other home. The promised one in the dark of the woods. The home you have to stray from the path to find. The home that you think might kill you at first, but then you realize the only way out of the nightmare is through that home. And after, when you face whatever it is you need to face in there. After, when you open the door and step back out of that home, the world is colored an octave higher. And you know the home is yours now. It is a safe place because you went in there alone. And now you'll never be alone again.

It was a whirlwind romance. I admit it. To meet and get married all within the space of a year. It was crazy. Certainly not smart. But how was I to know things would get this bad, that she'd become this out of control. I'd had relationships before. I knew men and women were different. Sometimes, I'd even thought they were from different planets. But Irena was a whole other level of strange.

"My cells are awake with longing," she'd said this past Saturday afternoon. I'd just returned from a workout at the local gym, so I was feeling pretty good. She'd been painting in the art room I'd set up for her when we first moved to L.A. A little room off our bedroom, well, actually her bedroom. I'd moved to the living room couch for the past month. "My cells are awake with longing." That's how she greeted me. No hello. No how are you or how did the workout go. I mean what are you supposed to say to that?

The truth is we barely talked anymore. I didn't know what to say to her. She rarely spoke, and when she did, it was statements like that, or "I dream myself into rain that falls over forests of melody." She said that to me the other night, or something like it. I don't really pay attention anymore. I don't know what to say, so I guess I really don't listen. She tells me that. She says I don't listen. It's true. So instead of listening that night I went about making myself a smoothie as I usually do after a workout. She kept on painting as if I wasn't there.

Halfway through my smoothie the thought hit me that maybe she was trying to communicate through her paintings. They were scattered all over her art room. Most of them were of cats. Big cats. Small cats. Cats together. Cats alone. You name it. But lately she'd shifted to landscapes. Not your average, everyday landscapes either. Not the kind you'd buy in the local art store. Or at least the kind I might buy. These were empty nightmarish landscapes, mostly drawn with charcoals, though sometimes she added dabs of blues or dark green color. No cats. No animals of any kind in fact. Most of them were of forests. Sometimes there was a lake or a river hidden deep in the forests with fog rising off the top of it, obscuring anything that might live there. In those paintings, the branches of the trees along the river or lake hung low like they wanted to touch the water but couldn't. Like they were unable to despite their longing. The landscapes seemed terribly sad to me. There was one I'll never forget. An old stone well set smack in the center of a small clearing. The stones were cracked and covered with moss like the thing had been there in that place forever. And big, dark trees stood all around it, as if they were guarding it. You could see the faint outline of a cottage beyond. But that wasn't what caught my eye. It was the well. I couldn't stop looking at it, as if it was calling me, as if it wanted me to peer down into its depths.

And that's when I remembered Luna, my childhood cat. I hadn't thought about her in forever. She loved being outside. We couldn't keep her in the house. If we tried, she'd sit in front of the door, meowing to get out. She wouldn't stop until you opened it for her. I'd test her sometimes to see how long she'd keep it up. It didn't matter if it was one hour or two hours or more, she'd always win. I didn't like to let her out because she loved climbing, and every time I'd let her out, she'd climb one of the many trees we had in our backyard. Every time she got herself up a tree, she'd be afraid to come down. And then I'd hear her meowing from high in the branches. She'd do it all day until I rescued her.

What drove me crazy, though, wasn't necessarily that she'd get herself stuck in the tree, it was that when I tried to rescue her, which she clearly wanted, or else why meow incessantly and pace the branch looking for a way down. When I tried to rescue her, she'd cling to the branch with her claws or worse try to get away and get herself stuck higher in the tree. She wanted to be rescued, but then wouldn't let me do it. It was like she didn't understand that I was there to help. Or maybe that she really didn't want to come down.

Maybe deep inside there was a part of her, a small part, but a part of her nonetheless that wanted to stay up in that tree, that wanted to go higher still.

That's what came to me when I looked at Irena's landscapes, when I looked at that well. You didn't know what was down there in that darkness. There was no way of knowing. The only way to know was to go down inside it, and I sure as hell wouldn't do something like that. Most normal people wouldn't. I don't really know who would. Maybe people like Irena. Maybe she'd do it. After all we've been through, it wouldn't surprise me. There's a big difference between normal people, people like me, and people like her. No wonder it was so hard for people to know each other, to trust each other, even when they needed each other so badly.

I stood in the doorway of her art room, watching her. "Irena," I said, more a plea than anything. I didn't want to do what I now knew was inevitable. "Irena," I said again.

It took her a few moments before she looked up from her work, but when she did it was as if she looked through me, as if she were unable to see the thing I was and so had to focus on something past me, something more stable, more solid. That scared me, too. What object, what thing did she see beyond me that was more real than me. That scared me as much as the well.

"I didn't want it to be like this, Irena," I said. "I didn't want it to end this way." I paused, started to step into the room, then held myself back, my hand on the door frame. "I didn't want it to end at all. You must believe that, Irena."

She went back to painting again, yet her gaze remained fixed on me, as if she'd finally seen something she could understand, something she could paint. "Hold still," she said. "Will you, dear? Can you remain like that for me a moment longer?"

I did as she said. How could I not when it seemed clear that maybe this would be our one moment of connection. I don't know how long I waited there like that. It didn't seem to matter. It may have been a minute. Maybe an hour. Caught between the desire to escape and the desire to glance just once at the painting, to see the landscape she found in me. To understand something about myself, something about us, maybe something I'd never understood before. In the end, like Luna, I chose the far less terrifying option of flight. I went straight to Alice. And from there we went to see Dr. Judd. The doctor would be more likely to take the word of two with a decision this serious.

# ALICE

*One, two, be loyal and true.*

I'm out of bread, and I need onions as well for the pasta I'm making. The grocery store is a few blocks from my apartment, and it's such a lovely evening. It's always a lovely evening in L.A. And who says nobody walks in L.A. I look to the moon. It's full tonight, and I wonder how it can be the same moon I knew in Illinois, that moon that could only reflect prairie, while this moon watches over this lovely city. Was it only a year ago that I was a nobody in Illinois and now I'm a few steps away from being Mrs. Oliver Reed.

*Three, four, always ask to know more.*

You have followed me all my life, little moon. I searched the skies for you as a child before I understood who you were, who I was. Then in my fourteenth summer, while I lay with my boyfriend on the hood of his car, all tucked in with pillows and blankets, you showed me. You showed me as you rose enormous in the night sky, an orange moon, a harvest moon. You showed me what it meant to reflect the sun. How you could be bigger than the sun and never need reveal your own light. You showed me how to reflect the light of others, particularly men.

*Five, six, be cheerful and warm—no tricks!*

Thank you, moon. That was a great gift. Thank you again and again. I can look back now and see myself inside the pattern of your reflected light. Oh, the change didn't happen overnight. I was a slow learner. At first, I tried to redeem men with other men. It took me time to realize the goal was not to let them into your orbit, not to let them pull me into theirs. Distance was essential if you were to be the perfect reflector of light. The goal is not to be seen. The goal is to give nothing away.

*Seven, eight, clean and attractive makes a date.*

O moon, the only arms I feel truly safe in are yours. They're long, and they hold me like no others. At the end of the world there will only be a woman and you. And dark on top of darkness until it makes a kind of light. O moon, sometimes I see myself in you, as if you, too, know this pain. And then I think of course you do. This pain is ancient. This pain rose on the first night of the world. And you rose with it. And with it the first woman gave birth. And with it our loneliness, our longing, was born.

*Nine, ten, let's start over again!*

A tremor of birds takes to the sky. What was that noise? There was a noise behind me. I'm sure of it. I take a few steps, my heels clicking along the pavement. I stop. The echo of my steps comes back to me from around the corner.

I walk again, faster this time. Then stop. Footsteps matching my own. I'm not alone.

Smile. Always smile. Never get mad. Or sad. Or afraid. Never.

I walk again, listening. The steps follow. My own steps follow me. I'm sure of it now. I stop, look behind me. Somehow the sidewalk seems narrower, the shop walls leaning in, casting long shadows under the light of the moon. I catch a glimpse of something moving in those shadows. The self I buried on that summer night of my fourteenth year. I can see her white dress, the red floral pattern on it. Impossible. But what else could it be? How much farther until the grocery store? Another block, that's all.

Be helpful. Be clean. Be honest. But don't be too honest.

Choose clothes that make you look good, but not too good.

Be alluring but not too forward.

My mantra keeps me safe. *One, two, be loyal and true.* My mantra keeps my own light hidden. Something like a growl sounds above me. I break into a run. I didn't mean to, but it's as if I can't stop myself, as if some primal fear has taken hold. *Three, four, always ask to know more.* But not in this case. In this case, I don't want to know. I thought my mantra contained the world, but it's only the world of men. Outside it, I'm lost. Outside it, I'm running alone down the street at night, chased by I don't know what. I'm almost there. The fluorescent light of the grocery calling to me. I'm almost there. Yes, I can see the store's fluorescence like the reflected light of the moon, offering a haven, a home.

# Dr. Louis Judd

Date of Referral: December 15, 2016

Patient: Irena Dubrovna
Patient DOB: 04/03/1991
Sex: Female
Race: Caucasian
Marital Status: Married
Emergency Contact Name: Oliver Reed

This document is to serve as a recommendation for involuntary commitment of patient, Irena Dubrovna for psychiatric treatment and care per court order ORC 5122.01(B). Patient to be remanded to Patton State Mental Hospital.

Reason for referral: Over the past month, patient's behavior has become erratic, showing increasing signs of being a danger to others and to herself. She has twice attacked her husband. He reports fearing for his life. I, myself, have been the victim of one such attack by the patient, as she accosted me in my office. It was only my own quick thinking that allowed me to escape with my life. Further, it is my considered opinion that she is in danger of taking her own life.

Primary Diagnosis: Severe Obsessive Compulsive Disorder. Patient obsesses over her fear of turning into a large, predatory cat, a panther to be specific. Compulsions take the form of avoiding any intimacy to the point that her marriage and relationships are compromised. The results of this repression of her true self and refusal to partake in intimate relations have led to violence against loved ones as the only possible release for emotions that might normally find their expression in other more appropriate ways.

Secondary Diagnosis: Major Depressive Disorder with suicidal ideations. Co-morbid depression is a common secondary diagnosis with extreme OCD. In this case the depression is so severe that her husband and loved ones fear she may harm herself.

Relevant Social Factors: I have met with patient's husband, Oliver Reed, and he concurs with my recommendation to have patient committed to the state mental hospital until such time as it is clear she will no longer be a danger to herself and to others. He has signed all necessary paperwork. Further, Irena's best friend, Alice Moore, accompanied patient's husband to my office. She also signed an affidavit attesting to her concerns regarding patient's state of mind. She affirms that she also felt threatened by the patient one evening on her way to the grocery store.

# Ending A

She sits alone in the corner like a piece of living art, listening to the clocks ticking all at once. She's decided that she's still ten inside. It's easier that way. Easier to be a child. No need to reign in desire. No need to fear intimacy. Now, even the spiders no longer undress before her.

Oliver and Alice are married with two children. A boy and a girl. She knows this, though no one has told her. It's the natural order of things. It's how the game is played. And she understands this, even if she can't articulate it. They live in a suburb outside the city. Not Santa Monica. Too bohemian. Not Beverly Hills. Too posh. But a relatively normal suburb like Irvine or Pasadena. He goes to work, and Alice plays the homemaker, at least until the kids are in kindergarten. But truly, she doesn't care about these things. She rarely thinks of them at all.

It's been raining all night. Pounding rain. The kind of rain that makes you think of the tropics, of monsoons. But now the rain has lifted. She walks to the window. She is sure she sees the place where the rainbow ends. It is lush and green there. Like a deep forest. She feels, for a moment, the desire to be lifted, to be drawn into the light. She wonders what mercy might come after; what mercy lies in that place where the sunset amends the rain. Then the moment passes, and she returns to her chair. She blows twice on each wrist and waits.

The nurse brings her a cup of water and her medicine. She takes it unthinkingly. The other patients shuffle back and forth. Once a week, the doctor checks in with her, and she answers his questions dutifully. Yes. No. Yes. No. When he leaves, she watches and waits. For what, she is no longer sure.

# Ending B

I stood in the doorway of her art room, watching her. "Irena," I said, more a plea than anything. I didn't want to do what I now knew was inevitable. "Irena," I said again.

It took her a few moments before she looked up from her work, but when she did it was as if she looked through me, as if she were unable to see the thing I was and so had to focus on something past me, something more stable, more solid.

"I didn't want it to be like this, Irena," I said. "I didn't want it to end this way." I paused, started to step into the room, then held myself back, my hand on the door frame. "I didn't want it to end at all. You must believe that, Irena."

She went back to painting again, yet her gaze remained fixed, as if she'd finally seen something she could understand, something she could paint. "Hold still, Oliver," she said. "Will you, dear? Can you remain like that for me a moment longer?"

I did as she said. I don't know why. Maybe because it felt like the closest thing to a connection we'd had over the past few months. I don't know how long I waited there like that. It didn't seem to matter. It may have been a minute. Maybe an hour. But the need that made me stop and wait there kept building until it felt like it was a bomb about to go off inside me. Like this moment was everything, and if I didn't act now, it would all be lost. Not just our marriage, but that something inside me, inside her would break. And there would be no going back from that.

So, I went to her and knocked the painting to the floor. The painting was of me, I think, but not quite me. It was a me dissected into cloud parts, my face floating away.

"That's not me," I said as I grabbed her by the wrist.

She dropped her paint brush and looked at me, eyes wide. Suddenly, I could smell the oil paint, the linseed and turpenoid. I could hear her breathing, and the faint beating of her heart. I could see her, and it was as if she were fire.

I pulled her by the wrist to the bedroom. She did not resist. I threw her face down on the bed, then pulled the restraints from the bedside table. She lay without moving, waiting for me, knowing what was coming. I tied her hands first, then her feet so that she lay spread-eagled before me. She said nothing, made no sound except a slight purring. I took the belt from my waist and spanked her. Her purring grew louder, as if it came from the center of her being. I spanked her again, and it was as if the only thing in my head was her purring.

I mounted her from behind. She arched her back to greet me. I could see already the transformation taking place within her. The hair sprouting from her body. The muscles rippling beneath the flesh of her back. Her nails long and sharp. I wondered if when we were done and I turned her over if I would recognize her.

Every lovemaking has to end, lest we go too easy with longing. And eventually so did ours, though we stayed in that bed all afternoon. The wild places her roar took me will forever echo in my mind. I'd never heard sounds like that before. I thought more than once that I, too, would become a panther, held captive as I was by her carnivorous desire. But no, that's another thing I learned that day. I'm as distant from the thing inside as the sun from the nearest star. I can't even begin to see the signs. It's better that way, I thought. Better to be blind to the thing within. I'd seen what the knowledge of it had done to Irena.

I didn't need to untie her. She easily burst through the ropes during her transformation. In the end, it was I who was lying face down, soaked in sweat on the bed. She stood over me on all fours, licking the sweat from my body, nudging me with her whiskered muzzle. Her feral breath hot on my neck and face. I turned to her then, unsure what I might find. Would she kill me? Dismember me there on the bed? How much of her human nature did she retain? At first, I couldn't find her. The rainforest of her eyes was too thick. All I could see was the dark glow of the panther above me. But then, I saw her, or at least the part of her I'd come to know, flickering deep in that forest. She was there, and she would not kill me. Rather, those eyes begged me for something else.

When night fell, we left our apartment. I didn't attempt to restrain her or put her on a leash. She climbed into the backseat of my car. I could feel her panting breath on me as I drove. Somehow, I knew exactly where to take her, as if all of this had been foreordained. Once we got to the zoo, I followed her. It wasn't easy getting over the wall, at least not for me. I was surprised at the sounds of the zoo at night. I'd always assumed it would be silent, animals sleeping. But it was quite the opposite. Or maybe it was the presence of Irena that stirred them up. So much life about me that I never realized was there.

At the leopard enclosure it was easy enough for her to leap in. I worried about her being accepted by the other cats. And at first, they paced around her, growling, wary. But as is the custom with most animals, eventually, they accepted her into their number.

I stayed all night that first evening, watching her, feeling closer to her than I'd ever felt, understanding for the first time what real connection was like. A connection where words were no longer necessary. A connection where each is allowed to become. Where becoming is a state and not an object. And though I couldn't spend every night there, I came back often. At first, my hope was always to see if I could still recognize the Irena that was, the Irena that had been. And I usually could. But as time went on, that mattered less and less. What became more important was just to watch her, to rejoice in the strangeness of her, the parts I didn't know, the parts I'd never known. And more, to understand and even, perhaps, appreciate that deep in the darkness within her, there were parts wild and strange I would never come to know.

I must admit I was surprised to see her when she stormed past my secretary and burst into my office. I'd been expecting something, but nothing this dramatic.

"Please, doctor," she said. "Don't do this! Don't send me away! They'll listen to you."

Before I stepped from behind my desk, I unlocked the drawer. I don't know why I thought of doing so. I don't think it was a thought. More an impulse. A warning from my unconscious. "Your husband and his friend made a very compelling case," I replied, walking toward her. "And I must say I agree with them."

"No," she shouted. "No. My husband doesn't understand me. No one understands!" She collapsed on the sofa and began sobbing. A flock of pigeons landed on the telephone line just outside the office window, making a racket.

I sat beside her, took her hand in mine. It's times like these when patients need a human touch. "There's only one way to break you free of your delusions, Irena." She looked at me then with wide eyes, not eyes of innocence, but of understanding. She blew twice on each wrist. I leaned in close, whispered "No more silly games, Irena," just before I kissed her. I pulled back to gauge her reaction, but found her eyes revealed nothing. It was as if they'd gone dead. I couldn't decide in that moment whether they were the flat eyes of the prey in the moment the cat has them by the throat, the moment they realize is their last, or if they were the eyes of the predator, the flat eyes of death. This time it was she who whispered to me as she leaned in for another kiss. "There's no escaping this world intact," she said, then kissed me with more force, more passion than I'd expected. Soon she was on top of me. Purring. Growling. Holding me to the couch by my wrists. She brought her face close to mine, opened her mouth, and I could swear I could see fangs just before she bit into my neck. I screamed and bucked against her. But still she held me firm. It was as if she had the strength of ten men. I didn't understand what was happening. Her face took on a different shade, darker, wider. Her eyes seemed to glow. She roared, arching her back as her body transformed above me.

When it was over, she crouched atop me, panting, staring into me with those horrible green eyes. She swiped at me with her claw, tearing into the skin of my chest. I feared for my life but strangely had given up the struggle. She shifted from my body and swatted at me again knocking me to the ground. I tried to stand and swooned. I must have lost more blood from my neck and chest than I thought. Still, she did not pounce, though she could have easily finished me. I remembered the times I'd seen my own house cat, Felix, play with a mouse. The patience as he watched it writhe and squirm. She waited, watching me from her perch atop the couch. When I didn't move, she growled at me, pawing at the air, as if pushing me to do something. At first, I didn't understand. Then it became all too clear. Slowly, I moved toward my desk, hoping I could make it before I lost too much blood. Slowly, she followed me, careful to keep her distance, but also, clearly, pushing me on.

When I got to my desk and reached inside the drawer, she growled again, crouching on all fours, ready to spring. I raised the pistol and fired just as she pounced. The last thing I remember were her teeth tearing into my neck, my blood mingling with hers.

# ENDING D

Isit downwind from the scents of so many of my brothers and sisters, spinning in the black trance of the ache and echo of myself. I wear green and sit on a bench, half-hidden by the thick foliage around me. The visitors walk by without noticing, except for the occasional child being towed by his or her mother who might look back for a moment to catch a second glance at this strange creature that reminds them of a distant part of themselves. But as soon as the little girl or boy looks back, the mother pulls the child along again. And I am forgotten.

Is there any distance between giving up and letting go? I don't know. I haven't found the answer yet. I take solace in the fact that there are more like me than I ever thought possible. We stroll about the zoo at dusk or dawn, when there are few visitors, and nod to each other in passing. That recognition is everything. The gaze that stops and sees into you. The sound of that can be heard for miles by the least of us. Occasionally, when no visitors are about, we'll stroll with each other arm in arm. During those times, we say nothing. We don't need to speak. It is enough to feel the other's arm in ours, to smell them beside us, feel the rhythm of our steps together. As we walk, we sometimes watch the sky, beyond which another sky flows. Or we turn to the forest that surrounds the zoo, beyond which another forest grows. What is reflected in the first, is transfigured in the second. We know this to be true. Nothing is ever really as it appears. Deep in the hidden corners of that second forest, that second sky, the sun does not reach.

But here in the zoo or anywhere where our kind congregate we don't need the sun. Each of us is a candle to the other. A single candle to light the other's darkness.

We never stay together too long. We know the candle lasts only a short time, and we don't want it to burn out and be lost forever. These, after all, are the limits of love. And you can no more understand me than I can explain myself to you. So, after we stroll the zoo, either alone nodding to each other, or together, arm in arm, we retreat to our own space where grass and flowers are invisible, where each scent grows green and time trickles away to nothing. Though I can't talk about these moments without betrayal of the place, without revealing the sacred location of this small house in the darkest corner of the woods, it is in these times I think this might be home. Or at least a place to stay for a while.

# P/I/E/R/T/E/E/N/R/A

I don't know why I'm writing. I don't believe we have anything more to say. Except I've been thinking more and more as I near the end of this novel about whether we would publish it. I'm honestly wondering whether we'll ever show it to anyone. And if we do, who do I say wrote it? You know how it is. People want things to be simple. Clear. They want an author. In short, they want a name. A persona. Preferably with a photo that makes the author look wise. So, whose name do I give them? Yours? Mine? Oliver's? Nastassja's? Alice's? Dr. Judd's? Simone's? And then what happens once there's this physical object in the world with a name on it. And you or I step into a bookshop and pick up this book and read these words. What will we think then? Whose words will we be reading? When you gave me these words, when I gave you these words, I had no idea they would turn into this book. You told me, "A free woman in an unfree society will be a monster." You told me that. Or maybe I told you that. It's all so confusing. And those words began this book. I had no idea this book, this object would get inside us the way it has. No idea this object would get inside you. That this object would become you. And you, me. I don't know. In fact, I'm no longer sure about anything. Except that maybe I've discovered (we've discovered) what it means to have longing. I mean to long for something so much you feel hollow inside because whatever is real in you has burst out of your chest like some monster. And that monster is you. Or is it me. Are we the monsters, Irena? Or are the monsters still inside, still trapped in their cages? I see you, Irena. And you see me. We see each other because we are each other. We know that now. But now we don't know what to do with this thing, this object, this book. We don't know what to do with this metaphor. Is it a lie like so many others? Is there a semblance of truth deep in the darkest of these woods we write? Maybe it's safer to let it be, to let it exist only on this hard drive where no one can see it. Once the book becomes an object in the world. Once it's out in the world sitting on a shelf somewhere, maybe the shelf of a college student. Maybe the shelf of a young Serbian woman who likes to draw pictures of cats in the zoo or the shelf of a sixty-year-old man who only wants to retire and play music. Maybe a bookstore shelf where it becomes a product people might buy. What might happen then? Nothing? Everything? What if this object makes its way inside someone else? And then something bursts out of them? Who is responsible then? It's all a bit much. And I'm done thinking. We're done thinking. Thinking leads to this, and we don't know what this is. What is this, Irena? I feel I can ask you now that you've been born, now that you've been delivered from me, now that you are your own self, another object existing in this strange world. I say again, what is this? You don't know either, do you? In that case, I have another question for you, for me, for us. Are you afraid of love, Irena? Are we afraid of it? I think, perhaps, I might be. A little. We might be. The world wants us to be afraid of it. The world is afraid of it. I mean, look what might happen if people loved each other, if people looked past the veil and really saw one another. I can't imagine what that place might be like, or maybe I don't dare to, we don't dare to, because it would be so beautiful. And sometimes beauty is painful. We know that now, too. The simple fact is that we were born into a fearful world, and if we grow up in such a fearful place, we can't help but be afraid. And we know why the world is afraid, don't we? I think everyone knows. They just don't want to say, or maybe they can't say because that's scary, too. Because if we were to love, to truly love, then you would be set free. Then I would be free. We would be free. But mostly you. And that's a scary thought. That's why we have cages. To contain that thought. To contain the possibility of that thought. If that's the case, I'm not sure there's anything left except to say thank you. Thank you, Irena. I don't know why I said that. Thanking you like that. It felt necessary. Maybe even like it was the main reason for writing this book in the first place.

To thank you. To give you voice. To give me voice. I must admit, I'm a little frightened, Irena. I know I'm harping on this…this idea about the book getting published, becoming an object in the world. I know what will happen despite my best efforts. I'm the one they'll call the author. Even though it's not true. Even though we've both always known these words are yours. Or at least ours. I suppose it's all for the better. We've always been trapped between wanting to create art that is accessible and creating art that reveals the part that is not normal, or that we tell ourselves is not normal, the thing inside that we won't let others see. That's why it's been so difficult to sit and write. Because there's no way out of that trap. Oh, and there's one more thing, Irena. One more thing I want to know before we go. Are you what awaits me? Am I what awaits you? I hope so. If you're there somewhere in my future, in our future, even if it's in my dreams, then we can go on. Then I can go on. I know we can. I'm certain of that. Are you certain, too?

# DREAM MEMORIES OF THE FIFTY FOOT WOMAN

Irena Dubrovna

*We are stories telling stories*
  —Fernando Pessoa


*I'm half living my life between reality and fantasy at all times.*
  —Lady Gaga

# UC San Diego, Medical Center

she lies in bed in the emergency wing, tubes running out of her arms, her nose, her mouth, she is forty-six, no one visits her, forgotten, her life one long process of forgetting, first the beauty pageants and television shows, then Hollywood, then, the doctors and drug companies, and the lawyers, too, all those visits, those x-rays, those letters, gone, so many people she thought she knew, so many people she, too, has forgotten, and now, she's no longer sure she exists at all, now, only the machine exists, the pinging machine that tells her she's supposedly alive, the machine that reminds her she's not yet ready to climb the steps to the moon, the sky beyond her shuttered window a doubtful gray, the sky like a candle flickering, leading her back to what she knows, what she's always known, and so she raises a hand just to see if she can, it's bigger than a mountain, as enormous as a storm, she could tear the roof from this place, smash the doctors and nurses with her fist, this, too, she understands, she could grab the lawyers and squeeze them until they pop, but she cannot smash the pain, the pain is eternal, the pain is fluid, striking at her like a flame, sometimes orange, sometimes red, sometimes green or blue, always there is pain, that dull rat heading blindly for the bone, it is eternal, it is the only thing that is real, that and the machine, and life is an illusion, a waterfall of illusion, and pain is a river rising from that waterfall, pain for how long now? she's no longer sure, twelve years, twenty years, one hundred, does it matter anymore? each suicide a successful attempt at sublimation, and oh, how long she's contemplated suicide, at least as long as the pain, that sweet kiss of death, almost as long as she's been taking those calcium supplements, the pills loaded with lead, 190 ppm to be exact, the toxicology report confirmed what she'd already suspected, what no one believed, not a single doctor out of the dozens she'd visited over all those years, the doctors who told her it was in her head, that her pain was psychosomatic, not the lawyers who told her to stop complaining, told her the tabloids would have a field day with her if she went public with her insane conspiracy theories about being poisoned, not the movie producers, not the directors who told her she was unstable, that she'd become "difficult to work with," not the friends who wondered why she walked with a cane at age forty, who wondered why she couldn't seem to land a part anymore, the friends who wondered why she'd let herself go, she'd been such a looker, they told her, she was the cat's meow, they said, and look at her now, hunched over, hair falling out, using a cane for Christ's sake, you're a bit dramatic, aren't you? they said, it can't be all that bad, her friends were the cruelest cut of all with their inability, no unwillingness to see this leviathan in her belly, this thing that had invaded her, this thing that had become her, that she'd become, you think I'm drunk, don't you, she tells them, you won't believe me, I'm not drunk, she says, but is that her voice? from what body does she speak? she's no longer sure, Mary Jane Hayes, or Allison, Allison Hayes, actress, movie star, *femme fatale*, unstable woman, the woman she's been for so long, I'm not drunk, you think I'm drunk, don't you, you won't believe me, or is it that other voice? Nancy Archer's, the voice from the role that made her famous, yet one more thing she couldn't control, why that role, why not Georgina McCray, the arrogant southern belle brought low by Raymond Burr's Yancey, why not that role, it was her best, wasn't it? that was the role that should have garnered her awards, and isn't that role also her? Mary Jane, Allison, Georgina, Nancy, they are all the same woman, what we read, what we watch, becoming what we are as much as lived experience, we are a multitude of stories, we are stories telling stories, it may be all we are in the end, it may be all we are reduced to when the body is gone, the rest, mere facts crumbling to dust and ashes, dust and ashes, and so we tell and re-tell the same stories over and over again, and it's all we can do, she understands that all too well, now that the end has come, and she certainly lived *those* lives, as much as she's lived her own, I'm not drunk, you think I'm drunk, don't you, you won't believe me, and so she goes on memorizing her lines, and *her* lines, and how many cuts did they do for each scene in that godforsaken film? she's imbibed Nancy Archer more than she ever drank, more than all those calcium pills she popped every day for twelve years, or was it a hundred, she's swallowed Nancy's thoughts, gulped down Nancy's lived experience inside her, the same way she took in the radiation from the three-hundred and forty X-rays she underwent, the three-hundred and forty X-rays doctors ordered to locate the pain they told her was non-existent, the three-hundred and forty X-rays that gave her the leukemia that is the reason she's now lying in a coma in this hospital bed in San Diego with tubes connecting her to the pinging machine, the ghost of her life standing by the window, the ghost of her life unspooling like a film reel, first the waterfall, then the river, hollowing out this room in which she sits, and now the ghosts are here leading her to what? a beginning, an ending, some place in the middle, she's not sure, she only knows the time for fear is over

**the** sphere looms large before her, looking at her as if it were trying to break something inside, as if it were telling her something, something she's known before, something she's always known, and she's standing on a dirt road in the middle of the desert, and she doesn't know how she got here, how she arrived at this place, middle-aged, half-drunk, and only recently released from the mental hospital her husband put her in, a husband? really? is she married? how can that be? Allison Hayes was never married, though Mary Jane was, at least she thinks so, that avatar from another life, a quick marriage when she was oh so young, followed by an annulment, just as quick, and Hollywood agents to rewrite the rest of her history, Mary Jane lost in the flame of the poem of life so that Allison Hayes could be born, hypocrite woman, and how did you let her go, Allison? how did you release all that she was, all she'll ever be, until she's gone, nothing more than desert dirt, and you did it, and then she remembers the question that set her driving out of town, it wasn't anything her husband had done, not anything the doctor had said, she'd been sitting on the park bench in front of the clock tower on fifth, staring up at the clock, watching, waiting for the minute hand to move, every minute is a negotiation with my body, she thought, every minute a negotiation, and then the thought that set her on the road in the middle of the desert—how is something, when it is removed from that which made it something else, how is something itself again? she was no longer herself, she'd come to that realization while sitting before the clock tower, something, let's call it a creature, had slowly pushed its way out of her chest, out of the cocoon of her body, and now she wants to know, is she the creature or the body it left behind? that's the question that plagues her, that's the question that set her out on this desert road, and it's not irrelevant, and she will be met, something will meet her, here in the desert or at the clocktower, something hangs in back of her still, something she can't see, and it's heavy, and she feels it like a weight, a weight hanging on her, or perhaps a weight growing inside her, and then she wonders, what if it's pure energy? what if she can find a way to release it? would it become, would she become, pure light? or simply another something? and what caused this split, this rupture within? was that important? surely it was important to understand the reasons so it wouldn't happen again, or maybe it had to happen again, maybe it had happened to her many times before, and she was unaware, to be a camera without film— and yet recording, that was her, she was like a camera—the lens open, the machinery whirring and clicking, but no film inside, at least that had been her up until now, up until this point in the desert where she stands face to face with a giant sphere, a smooth, white sphere the size of a house, and again she wonders, how did I get here? and then she thinks, it's her body, isn't it? this thing, this sphere, it's her body, the thing she left behind in front of the clock tower, it's her body like the flowers she planted in May, and now it's September, and they remain flowerless, has she learned anything from that experience? does she understand anything other than the fact that moments ago she was sitting in front of the clock tower, wishing to die, does she understand anything other than that she sat there for hours, afraid of what might happen if she moved, would she travel further toward or away from herself? and she thinks, I've been alive for forty-six years, and I have no idea where I'm going, and now she's here, in front of the giant, white sphere, in front of her body, without a face, or at least what she thinks may be her body, the thing she left behind, and so she exits her car and cautiously steps toward the thing, the body/sphere, and she is pulled by something she doesn't understand, and the body/sphere seems to quiver in the sun, as if it's alive, and so she stops, afraid to go any further, no, no, no, she screams, shaking her head, as if she could stop what's going to happen next, and she knows now that life up to this point has been a counterfeit, a dream, and she understands that now she is alone, more than alone in the middle of the desert, and now, the door stands before her, the door in the sphere, in the middle of the desert, and all she need do is knock, and so she tries, but her will is not enough, she cannot raise her own arm, and now the body/sphere reaches a hand toward her, a giant hand, a hand reaching through the door in the sphere, a hand bigger than a mountain, as enormous as a storm, and it is reaching for her, and there she is, standing immobile, unable to stop from happening what she knows must happen, what she wants to happen, in spite of herself, and then the hand touches her, caresses her, or is it shaking her, even as she screams, and then it tries to hold her, and she's no longer sure whether it's her hand or another's that reaches to her from the body/sphere, whether it's her hand or another's that is trying to hold her, no matter, she's changed her mind, she doesn't want this, and so she turns and runs back down the road in the middle of the desert, the sun falling behind her like clockwork

**sixteen**, breasts round, and legs long, and she's already begun the string of beauty pageants that will lead to her being discovered, music led her there, Rachmaninov's Piano Concerto No. 2 in C minor blows her way, and so she followed its scent through the pageant circuit, it is her favorite song, the one she spends what has seemed like most of her young life struggling with on the piano, but now she has it, or rather it has her, it has tapped into the rage within, the rage she'll never let out on her own, and in so doing, it's changed the course of the river of her life, it's given her a talent to go with her beauty, it's given her a reason to go on, and now she's a shoe in on the pageant circuit, everyone says so, but there's just one problem, the problem is there's something growing inside her, and she doesn't know what it is, she thinks it's a sphere, a sphere inside her, and no one can know, and she feels it all the time, tucked up under her ribcage just below her heart, she feels it like the ache that lingers after a rain, like the crescent of golden wheat over a field, like ribbons of light in the nighttime sky, in other words, it's like something she doesn't comprehend but nevertheless must carry within her every single day, and each day it grows within her, like each idea, each feeling becomes the thing, the sphere, and soon it will speak to her, she knows this, she plays the Rachmaninov to quiet the sphere, to silence it, that's what the Rach does for her, and she is not ready, she tells herself, not ready for what the sphere contains, what it will do to her, she tells herself, she'll be ready after she wins the pageant, after she makes a name for herself, after she's become an actress, and then the pageant arrives, Miss America, 1949 in Atlantic City and the judges tell Miss District of Columbia that her Rachmaninoff is not acceptable, they tell her it is too angry, too aggressive, and they want her to do something more becoming of a young woman, so they suggest she sings, perhaps "Over the Rainbow" or "Swinging on a Star," perhaps she'd like to sing a song like that, something with hope and just a hint of melancholy, and then her cousin Tommy arrives to support her, Tommy, her favorite cousin who is the same age as her, Tommy who she used to sit by the river with and just talk about nothing and everything, and so she hugs him in the hotel lobby, she can't help it, that's who she is, how she was made, lead with love, she's always told herself, but no one told the Miss America pageant committee that, and that was her mistake, and so she gives her cousin a bear of a hug, a hug so big the press can't miss it, and, of course, they have a field day with it, and the judges disqualify her for "publicly fraternizing with a male," though they never told her she was disqualified, because if they told her, that might hit the papers, and that might create a scandal, and so, they simply refuse to move her forward in the contest, and so, she doesn't even place in the top fifteen, she who was favored to win only a month before, but she is not the "good girl" the press wants her to be, and certainly not the "good girl" the pageant committee wants her to be, and so she complains, and so she talks to the press about the secret disqualification, she tells them about the secret meetings in back rooms, about what the girls are supposed to do and not supposed to do if they want to win, but no one believes her story, you think I'm drunk don't you, all of you, I'm not drunk, I'm not…you don't believe me do you? any of you? Nancy is that you? have you been with her from the beginning? are you the giant moving within the sphere within her body? and so this, too, is the start of her hearing voices, the start of her splitting and becoming so many others, and so this is where Mary Jane dies, she dies just after the beauty pageant, she is no longer that person, she never wants to be that person again, the person no one listens to, the person people control, the person people tell things to like, Rachmaninov is too angry, too aggressive, or, fraternization with males is not allowed, and so she is now Allison Hayes, and Nancy Archer, and so many others, and yes, she's always been them, always been Nancy Archer,

Nancy can do what she wants, Nancy is a millionaire, Nancy is the giant who strides across the desert, but she is not Nancy yet, at least not completely, and there are so many, many branches the river takes, so many, many rivulets into the future, only some of which we can know, and so, strangely, the beauty pageant winner, Jacquelyn Mercer, will die of leukemia at the age of forty-nine in an L.A. hospital just three years after Allison dies of the same disease a couple hours south in San Diego, and the similarities don't end there because Jacquelyn and Allison will also both marry and divorce their high school sweethearts in the year after the pageant, Allison's marriage, when she was still Mary Jane, annulled, expunged from the record, but not the pain of it, not the grief of it, the grief, a sphere whose door swings open, hand beckoning in welcome, another giant hidden within, rising from its crouched hiding place, the giant whose exhalations form the air we breathe, our lungs are pocked with it, endless circling, endless revolution of dream to anguish to flame

**emptiness** spills into her, filling the sphere, like a swarm of bees, a liquid, crawling, shimmering swarm of bees, shaping and reshaping itself inside of her, emptiness spilling to find I, to find I-Who-I-Am again, and so she screams, Harry! Harry! Harry, help me! while her husband sits in the diner with that floozy Honey Parker, and so the sheriff says, just be calm, Mrs. Archer, be calm, you don't believe me do you? any of you? the refrain of her life, like a poem, a mantra within her, and the sheriff, guiding her with his hands, controlling her with his strong hands, I'll believe you, Mrs. Archer, just be calm, I'll believe you, now sit down in the police car, honest woman who wants to be believed, she may as well want the moon, and so let her rest, she needs time to rest, that's all, time in a quiet place where she can regain her sanity, where she can relearn the alphabet, relearn the world, and so she wakes up in the mental hospital, strapped to a bed for her own good, filled with hostile longing, or at least that's what they tell her, filled with pills, or at least that's what they give her, and she tells them she's only filled with emptiness, a swarm of bees, she tells them, and they say that's further proof she belongs there, and she says there's no there, anymore, no here, and each day is winter and more winter, and now the language of sphere opens within her, the language of dying in the simplicity of a day, the language of what happened? something small at first, something growing where the palm of her hand rests just below the ribcage, that's where the shame is, that invisible barrier deep in the mineral dark, and so she turns and turns and turns it over, little acorn of shame for the little girl who didn't practice the right songs, the little girl who tried to mimic her mother, to enter a room the way she entered a room, to laugh the way she laughed when there was an uncomfortable silence, to paint her face into the semblance of desire, and when her mother left the room, she left her flesh to follow her, she filled her shadow, filled her steps, and still she was doomed to fail, it's the metaphysics of desire, the desire to be something else, someone else, the desire to be loved, and cruelty is a mother leaving a room, leaving a shadow of desire for her daughter to fill, and so she cannot move, cannot leave her bed, but she can look out the window, and it's late afternoon, the oak on the lawn casts a shadow, the oak has no leaves, perhaps it never had leaves, but it has a shadow, an enormous shadow, spreading across the lawn, and the shadow climbs the wall of the hospital and enters her room, and the sphere grows inside her until it feels as if it will burst out, and she's sure it is the only thing that can fight off the shadow, the shadow that is like a stone waiting for some hopeful breath, the shadow that is like a child waiting for the touch of its mother, and she knows this, and she dreams she is reading the book of her life, it's a book of poems, and she imagines a poem that isn't there, what might it look like? she wonders, would it look like the battle between sphere and shadow? but the dream is interrupted by the sound of footsteps, the doctor enters, there's nothing physically wrong with you, Mrs. Archer, it's all in your mind, and so she reaches into her mouth, stuffs her fist down her throat, searching, searching until she pulls the sphere out of her and throws it on the floor where it becomes a black hole, it becomes the edge of the universe, and now there's a darker darkness inside the shadow, and she peers into it, it is not what she expects, not darkness exactly, or at least not any darkness she understands, and this is something else entirely, she thinks, it is a wet, crawling darkness, and so she unfastens the straps that hold her to the bed, then takes off her wedding ring because she is Nancy Archer, not Allison Hayes, not in this dream, not at this moment, and she throws the ring in the hole, and she listens for it to hit bottom, but she hears nothing, the hole is bottomless, and so she takes off her hospital gown and throws it in as well, then she strips the bed and throws the sheets in the hole, then she takes her pain and sets it delicately on the bed, and finally,

finally, she, too, jumps in the hole, and as she's falling, she spreads out her arms so that it feels as if she's flying, and it's not a bad way to die, she thinks, she's thought of worse ways, many, in fact, there are so many worse ways to die, and she's almost acted on them, too, so many times, so many times staring at the bottle of pills and the glass of vodka, so many times searching for the rope or the plastic bag to tie around her head, but now she is falling, and so she looks out of the hole as she falls, and she looks past the hospital ceiling and out to the sky, the brilliant, blue sky, and she listens, too, as she falls, and she hears only the wind in her ears, not the voice of her husband, not any more, not the doctors' and lawyers' voices buzzing, buzzing, buzzing, and only emptiness fills her, emptiness spilling into the sphere within her, a liquid, crawling emptiness spilling into her to find the woman-world-of-blood, to find I, to find I-Who-I-Am again

**here** is the apocalypse, one more in a series of many bad films, and so she's Allison again, acting opposite a talking mule in her first feature, *Francis Joins the WACs,* and the world of the set is white and still, and look at Donald O'Connor marching up and down, back and forth, making sexual innuendos with the women whenever he gets the chance, and the plummeting of her own heart is like a stone in a pool, and the rings spread out encircling her, the rings spread out farther and farther back through time, back inside the time with her mother and the desire for her touch, and she rolls her eyes because she can't imagine a worse fate than being in a movie, she hates movies, and yet it's the career she's chosen, why? she doesn't know, perhaps it has to do with her mother, doesn't everything, and now she's losing days to seasons she'll never know, and that's when she sees her co-star, Julia Adams, fresh from her role in *Creature from the Black Lagoon,* and the clouds peel back like a pool cover, revealing a sky blue and bottomless, and she begins to cry, and she doesn't understand why, at first, she feels the crying in her head, but then she realizes it's coming from her chest, it's coming from deep within the sphere, her sadness is the world entire, and it is within her, and now everything is uncertain, now, she has become formless, and she doesn't remember what they said to each other, or even if they spoke at all, and none of this is real, Frances the Talking Mule says, nudging her in the behind with his muzzle, and she thinks she must be going crazy because here is a talking mule, standing around as if he owns the place, but then she remembers of course he's the star of the film, the star of countless films, not Donald O'Connor, not even Julia, and then he speaks again, saying, none of this is real, but it is real, she thinks, as real as anything she's ever known, the dark line of Julia's face, that's real, and the eyes free of the inconvenience of having to be understood, those are real, too, but otherwise, the mule's right, you know I am, he says, stomping his hoof three times, and from that point on she does whatever she can to get away from the mule and to occupy the same space as Julia, and she knows if she gets close enough, she can hear Julia's music, Chopin, Nocturne Op. 9 No. 2 in E flat major, it's all she needs, all she's ever needed, and she wants to sit at the piano again for the first time since the Miss America pageant, and she feels like herself again for the first time since she can remember, but the problem is she's a minor character in the film and a minor character in Julia's world, and so she tries to map a path to Julia but finds that she no longer knows which path means going forward and which means going back, and

Donald is never far away, and he can't seem to get enough of Julia either, and then it happens, the unthinkable happens, because one night when filming goes later than usual, she suggests a midnight stroll before bed, something to work off the stress of the set, and Julia, to her surprise, agrees, and halfway through the walk she thinks she's going to die because she can't stop shaking, she's shaking so bad that Julia becomes concerned, it's not even cold out, it's summer in Los Angeles for God's sake, and Julia puts her arm around her as they walk, talking of their shared love of music, Julia's childhood in Arkansas and Allison's in West Virginia, and they laugh about how they each changed their names, a symbol of a new life, and how those old names said so much about their old lives in Arkansas and West Virginia, how Julia was born Betty May and of course Allison was Mary Jane, and how they both came up through the beauty pageant circuit, and how Julia was four years older than Allison, but she would live nearly fifty years longer, and though they didn't know that last part then, they felt it in the sharp stones and the dirt they walked over, though they didn't fully understand it and couldn't articulate it, they felt it when Allison stepped on a particularly nasty rock, breaking her sandal, *where are you going? where are you going?* the road said, and *how will you get there when you hold all your pain in the sphere? how will you get there when you're standing inside your pain?* and who knows, perhaps only Allison heard it, perhaps only Allison understood because her mother had talked of her own gift of divination, and perhaps Allison had inherited it, but we'd like to think Julia heard it, too, we'd like to think she was that kind of person, the same kind as Allison, but no matter, it's time to move the story on, to keep it moving, just as Allison and Julia are moving down the path to a place perhaps neither of them can imagine, and at one point, Allison is shaking so bad, Julia takes her in her arms, she's shaking so bad that Julia takes her and turns her so that they stand face to face, inches from each other, and it was like falling, Allison would later remember, as if we fell into each other, and she knows it is cliché, but her first thought is that she didn't know it could be like this, and she's embarrassed by the banality of that thought, but that doesn't make it less true, there can be truth hidden down deep inside the biggest cliché, just like there is sadness and grief hidden deep in the sphere inside every person, so deep we almost never can touch it, almost never open the door to let it out, and she's kissed men before, many times, she thinks, but nothing like this, nothing like this warm and tended fire, nothing like this song filled with . . . with what? she doesn't have time to think because Julia pulls her into a garden, a garden filled with trees she hasn't even noticed, and she pulls her into that small, curtained space free from the eyes of others, free from shame and guilt and so many things we keep locked in the sphere, and then she drops to her knees before Allison, and Allison doesn't know what to do, but she doesn't care, she feels like she's riding on a wave, or more like she's striding across the desert, a giant moving across a vast desert, and Julia lifts Allison's skirt, and she pulls off her panties, and buries her head between her thighs, and Allison almost falls again, but this time an oak saves her, and she backs into it, leans against it, and disappears for a few minutes in its embrace, disappears for a few minutes inside the giant striding across the desert, and mending takes these small precise steps, she thinks, yes, exactly these steps, and then it's over, and she opens her eyes, and Julia is gone, if she was ever there at all, and then she sees it, the mule's face watching her from within the wood, from within the garden, Frances the Talking Mule, watching them, watching *them*, because Julia was there with her, she was, she knows it to be true, and she feels it with everything within her, but Frances the Talking Mule opens his big mouth, nothing is real, he says again, not the long hallways of childhood fear, not the stale paper rooms of adulthood, and certainly not love, and so she grabs a rock and runs at him, but he doesn't budge, stubborn mule, he just stomps his hoof three times, and so she hurls the rock at him, it's real, it's real, it is real, she says, I'm not crazy, and Frances hoofs at the ground three times again, hold this night of wanting the rest of your life, he says, pack it deep in the sphere, and let it sustain you, let it grow within you until you are a god, and then let it break you, because that's what happens to gods

**and** now something wakening, its spiraling light rising out of her, what wild dawns, what feathers of gold, and she walks naked breathing in light, but they clothe her in a ragged and torn dress in her next film, *Sign of the Pagan*, a cloak she had not meant to wear, and they yank her by the hair, throw her to the ground, and she's the slave of Attila the Hun as played by Jack Palance, and they play the Huns as heathens who abuse women, who take many wives, not like the Christians who worship their one wife, and she gets flashes of another life where she has a husband of her own, if you only showed me once that you really cared, Nancy says to her husband as he gaslights her, as he plots to drive her insane, I'd do anything for you, Harry, she says, I don't know, maybe it's me, maybe I . . . but she doesn't want these memories because she's wakening, because she's seen the early morning sky, and she wants to build the piano inside the sphere inside her, and she wants to hear Chopin again, to play Rachmaninov again, so why does she reach for the bottle of scotch? and why is she being dragged by her hair from one tent to another, when Julia taught her things, Julia taught her the perplexities of inner space, Julia cracked open the door to the sphere and told her not to be afraid, told her to step into it, but now she wakes to troubled breathing, and she touches at her ribs just above the sphere and winces at the sharp pain, and she looks in the mirror and sees the bruised and broken lips, and she vows that she'll sue that son-of-a-bitch, Palance, she'll sue the whole stinking studio because she's done with Universal, she's done with movies, and the way they dumb everything down, the way they trap you in the sphere of their own stupidity, and so she complains to the director, he hurt me, Doug, he's too rough, just look at my lips where that jackass kissed me, and I think he squeezed me so hard he may have broken a rib, but the director barely looks at her when he speaks, what did you expect? you're a slave girl, of course, Palance is going to be rough with you, it's called acting, get used to it, and so she turns to the producer, Albert Cohen, but he won't even agree to meet with her, and the next morning is worse because she can barely breathe, and now she's sure her ribs are broken, and now more scenes from another life flash before her eyes, her husband, Harry, carrying her up the stairs to bed, not because he wants to make love, but because he wants to drug her to sleep, why can't you be nice like this all the time, Harry? she says, and he smiles and the light dies within her, or rather, the light is sucked into the sphere inside her, the sphere which is quickly becoming a black hole, and never mind the piano now, the piano with its Chopin and Rachmaninov that comes like thunder opening the door to the sphere, no, now it's a black hole sucking her from the inside out, here Nancy, her husband says, this will make you sleep, and Harry gives her the pills, his hand around her wrist like a small cuff, and she thanks him, yes, she thanks him because all she wants to do is sleep, better to sleep than to fight, and she's tired of fighting, she's so tired, even though the fight has only just begun, but she doesn't know that, not yet, and so she travels cross-town to see a lawyer recommended by a friend, his primary qualification being that he's cheap, and already that breath, that breath like a wild animal that presages the coming of bad weather, already that breath by which every unspoken word is, and how can she speak the unspoken? how can she find the words? and though she doesn't know this, the same thing will happen sixty-three years later, when Allison is long gone, a train lumbering through time to the year 2017 when the voices of so many actresses will rise up, demanding to be heard, like birds on a trembling branch before a storm, and even then it will be hard, much harder than it should be, but now it's impossible, but now she is only one, and in this moment, this now, she has not yet seen the giant hand extending toward her, the hand that will open her to herself, open her to herself inside the sphere, the one she keeps locked tight filled with fear and her pain, and so, the lawyer pretends to listen, and so, he says he'll send a "strongly worded warning" to the studio and Mr. Palance, and of course, all that means is that he'll write a mealy-mouthed note that says without saying, "watch out for this woman," and she'll become branded as "difficult to work with," as "troubled," and of course that's what happens, and so, she stays on the train, tries to ride it through into the next life and the one after that, the life she is destined for in the image she holds of herself deep down in the farthest reaches of the sphere inside, and so sixty-three years later the birds will sit on the trembling branch, they'll sit cupped and quiet in their firm refusal to sing again

**and** when it comes it will feel like an unfastening, like opening a cabinet to forgotten things, and when it comes it will feel like the forgiveness of birds, like basking in autumnal light, and so she wants to be done with movies, she wants to move into the next stage of life, but what else does she know? and 1956's *Gunslinger* holds so much promise, and promises so much money, money which she needs after her failed lawsuits, and she is one of the two female leads in a story that showcases two strong, independent women, Erica, the saloon owner, and Rose, the sheriff's widow who takes over the mantle of sheriff in a lawless town, and she should have read the script because she didn't know the two strong, independent women would be pitted against each other, leave it to Hollywood to waste the only two decent roles for women by turning those roles into a mud wrestling match for its stars, and now is the moment they film the scene where Rose and Erica get in a fist fight in the bar, and Allison knows she can't afford to live this experience, to take this life inside her, and so she famously asks, who do I have to sleep with to get off this film, and that night, she takes home the entire script and reads it, though it pains her to do so because her character will hire a gunman to kill Rose, it's insipid, she thinks, she wants no part of it, two women who fight like men, who can't even talk to each other, two women who can't resolve their own dispute, two women who need to hire a man to get between them, just another menage-a-trois as far as she's concerned, another male sex fantasy masquerading as art, and so the next morning, she tells the director, Roger Corman, she wants off, of course you do, he replies, now get dressed and be ready for scene in ten, and then he walks away, already talking to his cameraman about the next shot, and her life flips again, and again she's Nancy Archer, standing in the living room of her mansion, the butler, Jess, looking on concerned as she drinks one scotch after another, and Harry rises from the couch, cigarette in hand, as she tries to talk to him, as she tries to talk with him, tonight, when I was driving home, there was this satellite, she tells him the story of her encounter with the sphere, but he just stares at her, just stares through her, oh please, Harry, you believe me, don't you, she says, and he places a hand on her shoulder, taking the drink from her with the other hand, then guiding her toward the stairs that lead to the bedroom, of course I do, sweetheart, of course I do, and he carries her to the bedroom like a strong man should, and her head is buried in his shoulder, and endless training in life makes her so good at being guilty, so good at falling into his strong arms, and

we must stop here because it is hard, so, so hard to watch
the way a life is shut away in strong arms, and we so want
to bring her home where her mother might touch her face,
where her mother might bring her inside the sphere, but
we know the truth, we know her mother is not capable of
such an act, she is not the kind of mother who can remind a
child about the different strings in their body, the way they
can play music, and so we must imagine that she will do it
herself, we  must imagine a person who is small and has
no strength, a person like Nancy Archer or even Allison
Hayes, we must imagine that person transforms the pain,
the grief, inside the sphere into a form of rage, what might
that person become? how big might they become? and we
try so hard to whisper this to her, to whisper the music into
her fevered dream, but she's worried she'll never know, but
she's stronger than she thinks, and she has it in her to act,
we whisper this to her, and maybe she hears, perhaps she
hears something, because the next evening on the set, as she
watches the red sun descend, its gigantic face disappearing
on the horizon, she understands that she must waken, that
it must begin here, and so, she rolls away the stone from her
tomb of sleep, and so, as Rose fires her gun, Allison takes
the opportunity to "fall" off her horse, and so she breaks
her arm, more pain, but it doesn't matter, what lies ahead
doesn't matter, it's all worth it, and she'll be unable to film

now for months, and that label, "difficult to work with," will grow, and it will follow her so that the good roles will soon dry up, but she doesn't care, because in a single gesture she's no longer a collaborator with others, in a single act, she's put herself on the path toward the center of the sphere, and she can feel it, through the pain, she can feel it, and she knows that everything up to this point has been nothing but rehearsal, her life a mere rehearsal, and she's provoked the deepest part of an imagined reality, and it's waiting, and maybe everything inside her, the pain, the grief, is nothing but the echoes of that reality, and she stands mute on the lip of it and what is a tale told by an idiot called? it turns out it's called *Count Three and Pray*, her third feature film, and her third portrayal of a femme fatale, this time a southern belle named Georgina Ducraine, who gets her comeuppance by having to marry and be abused by the town boss, Yancy Huggins, played by a particularly nasty Raymond Burr, and again she tells herself she's done after this film, but she needs this one last paycheck, she reminds herself that the lawyer bills from the last movie were too much, and so she spends as little time as possible on set, and she's studying piano again, and she threw away the bottles months ago, sobriety is reading the book with the shades drawn in her LA apartment, and she's learning to draw, something she's always wanted to do, drawing class every Monday night, in short, she's turning her life around, and she's drawing Julia, though she doesn't know she's drawing her, she talks to her, too, though she's not aware she talks to her, or at least not aware of how much she talks to her, *I want to draw you in your green robe, legs slightly open, I want to draw the curve of your mouth in the shadow of moons, feed me your dark-eyed loneliness, let me take it in myself and draw,* and she thinks about contacting her, asking her to coffee, or dinner, but she is afraid of where it will lead, or where it won't lead, she's afraid Julia doesn't think about her the way she thinks about Julia, with her, it's become an obsession, she talks to her, she sometimes finds herself imitating her mannerisms, small things like the way she moves her head when she laughs, or the way she'll turn to her with her entire being whenever she says the slightest thing, and then there are the dreams, she's come to think her dreams of Julia are the most real aspect of her life, in one dream, Julia is a sphere, a giant sphere with birds flying all about her, sparrows, she thinks, and Julia is swallowing the sparrows in great gulps, and she, Allison, is running toward the sphere with her arms out, pleading, begging, her mouth open, waiting for the chance to be filled, and certainly, there's nothing real about her job, she spends most of the day waiting on set, holding her breath, waiting for the planets to change their orbits, makeup and wardrobe people circling about her, then she gets up, says a few stupid lines, and sits down again for another hour, but at night, when she dreams, she's alive, but at night, she walks with Julia, nothing more, they just walk and talk, and it is enough to sustain her throughout the next day, and it doesn't matter that Julia is on her second husband by now, it doesn't matter that the tabloids talk of their undying happiness, it doesn't matter that during the day she's the loneliest person alive, just trying to avoid the

orbits of the makeup and wardrobe people, praying they
don't bruise the song of her body, in her dreams, she has
Julia to herself, that's all that matters, and then it happens,
she's in the supermarket checkout lane when she sees Julia's
pregnant belly on the tabloid cover, and by the time she
returns to her apartment, she's already begun to wonder if
their night in the garden was all a dream, if that night was
real or something she'd imagined, and then she's back in that
other life, the life she has not yet lived, but that will mark
her forever, no one thinks you're crazy, Nancy, Harry tells
her when she asks, though his face says it all, he definitely
thinks she's crazy, don't be so condescending, Harry, I know
what you're thinking, she replies, Dr. Cushing has just
ordered bed rest for poor Mrs. Nancy Archer because her
weak feminine constitution has been exhausted, and she's
back to drinking again, but who is it doing the drinking,
Nancy or Allison? does it matter? aren't they all her in the
end? we are what we read, what we experience, what we
see, what we dream, and so she's drinking with the TV
on, and the newscaster is talking about a satellite in the
desert, *ladies and gentlemen, this is KRKR-TV…Nancy Archer,
the former Nancy Fowler, heiress to the Fowler millions, and
owner of the fabulous Star of India Diamond has joined that
ever-expanding, international society of satellite seers,* where
is she? who is she? Nancy again? why always Nancy? what
is it about her that requires she play this part so many

times? *from the Archer's palatial home away from home, comes a report that Mrs. Archer has not only been seeing a sociable satellite, but it's inhabited as well, a thirty-foot giant! was he pink, with big ears and tusks?* does she detect sarcasm in the announcer's voice? of course, she does, and judgement, too, the world is full of women judged to be "hysterical," judged to be "temperamental," "emotional," and how does the news know what she's seen, what she's heard? how does it know what's in her head? does it know about the sphere, too? how it sits inside her, making it difficult to breathe? *well, maybe Mrs. Archer, who has recently been feuding with her husband, handsome Harry, has finally found a man from out of this world, a man who could love her for herself, come, come now, Mrs. Archer . . .* and she's off down the rabbit hole, no longer sure who she is or when she is, given her choices, who would not choose to disappear, the way our flesh disappears each night into dreams, we have done so ourselves many, many times, tucked ourselves away, hidden the truest part where no one could possibly find it, after all, who could handle the force of that part of us we keep hidden, that divine spark that would blind anyone who catches a glimpse, that diving toward the deep ocean floor, or running in great strides across a desert, that rising, rising into the summer night sky toward constellations, toward starlight swirling about like sparrows, waking you up over and over

**no** one witnessed that night in the garden except the trees, and maybe the mule, or did she dream him, too? their all too human cries of desire curtained off by the trees, no one could hear, no one could know the beauty of what she found there, only the trees heard, the blind and deaf trees, only they lived it, exactly as she had, only they remember it as she does, and so sometimes she imagines herself stepping into the bark of those trees, she imagines herself living there, tree-rings circling her arms until she becomes her own wilderness, and so she does this any time she needs strength whether it's in her real life or her imagined one, and the longer she lives, the more she realizes how little difference there is between the two, and how little she cares about that difference, and so when she steps into that other world again, that future world she's yet to fully visit, she steps out to it from within the tree, from within the place that gives her strength, she's going to be believed, she tells herself, she's going to make them listen, make the world see who she really is even if she has to crush the world beneath her feet to do it, I'm going out in the desert and find that thing, and you're going with me, Harry, she tells her husband, the one she doesn't yet have, the one that will only exist in a movie not yet made, but a movie that will come to define her, you're being ridiculous, Nancy, her husband replies, there's nothing out there, and she thinks of her strength again taken up as if she'd given the order, as if she'd again touched the sphere, you don't believe me, she says, well, you're wrong, you're all wrong, and she wishes for a flock of sparrows to be born in her mouth, she wishes for them to take off and swarm about her husband, handsome Harry, she wishes for them to blind him so that he can really see, and you're drunk, Nancy, her husband responds, why don't you try to sleep it off, and she walks away from her husband, walks out the front door toward the car, no longer caring if he follows, no longer caring if he listens, I have a strange feeling it's out there, somewhere, waiting for me, she says to herself, and why does she think it's out there? wasn't it inside, always within her own body? yes, but sometimes the way to the body leads through a desert, sometimes the way to the body leads through a place where reptiles cross slowly over sand and rocks like ancient ships, where they sleep or pretend to sleep as they move into and out of dreams, and so the darkness comes with the wind through the car window, the darkness and the emptiness that always accompanies it, and she doesn't expect anything, or rather, she doesn't know what she expects, maybe she expects everything, she knows only that she comes with eyes made to see, not to conclude, she is done with conclusions, only beginnings for her, and so she says nothing to Harry on the drive, and he doesn't speak to her, and it's as if the sphere has grown large between them, as if it now keeps them from seeing each other, forcing them to look out at the desert landscape, and it seems then, as she sits in that great silence, that the world with its dusks and dawns has nothing to do with her, that the world exists outside of her, wholly beyond her, or she outside the world, beyond it, and all she can do is look, look and watch with waiting eyes, well, now we've combed all through these hills, Harry says, there's nothing out here, just emptiness, and it's because he doesn't see, she thinks, because he can't see, because he is still in this world, and so he accepts its laws and what they write for him, he looks out into the emptiness and sees nothing, but she's not afraid of it, in fact, she needs it, though she doesn't understand why, and so she sees a rock here or there along the hard dirt, a bit of fallen tree trunk, exposed roots, anthills dotting the landscape, and ants busily working around them, she sees the black eyes of the ants, and the black pupils deeper still, though she doesn't know how she can possibly see that, mostly, she sees little distinction between the road and the dirt to each side, the dirt that extends into the dusk, making it difficult to see where the road ends and the horizon begins, the horizon she wants to open for her, to lead her to that new beginning, and she is led by the sleepwalker's stubbornness, taking refuge in this silence as if only here can she enter into the thing that she is, and in these moments, on this drive, she never wants to speak again, in these moments, she has stopped being a person, she is something wholly other, like the world, and so she sits in the car and waits while Harry drives, content to let time pass because she is no longer held within time, she simply wants to sit and wait and enjoy the great perfection of the emptiness of herself, and of the world about her, there's nothing out here, Harry says again, and suddenly she's brought back to herself, all that perfect emptiness gone, all the contentment erased, old habits die hard, she thinks, especially in a marriage where the roles are etched in stone, I'm sorry, Harry. I'm sorry, she says, crawling back to him, back into her guilt, the guilt she was born with, and that's when she sees it, rising out of the air before her, the white sphere, thirty feet in diameter, and she's back to herself, back to the creature she is becoming, and it's as if she's been born again, that's it, I told you I did see it, I was right, she says, I was right! it's real, it's real, it is real, I'm not crazy, I did see it, and we're left to wonder at how quickly she shifts, how quickly we can all shift, blown about as we are by our emotions, by things seemingly beyond our control, we won't dare use that cliché here of the caterpillar becoming a butterfly, that radical transformation that happens only once in a lifetime, no, we are beyond that, we know that every moment brings a new caterpillar, every second another change, another shift in who we are, how can we possibly keep up, and of course the answer is that we can't, it is beyond human scale, the answer is we must stop trying, is it because we, too, carry the sphere inside us, is it because we, too, are afraid to take the object of our desire inside us, to let go of the loneliness and pain and make room for something greater, and so she runs out of the car toward the thing, and as she runs, she thinks, I'm alive, I'm alive, and that's when the giant hand reaches for her, and it's as if she's a child again and her own mother is reaching for her, with a hand like a baptism, pulling her under, pulling her down to her knees, where nothing is lost, nothing is forgotten, and she knows then that though she has knelt in a thousand ways, she will learn a thousand more before she dies, and she knows that all that matters is the steep descent of knees, all that matters is mind dissolving into sand and dusk, and then she is gone something is growing with a shapeless murmur, something is growing inside her in tremulous pools, something is growing that reflects the sky above those pools, something that is no smaller than that sky, and it seems more than a billion years ago, that she met Julia, and still she dreams of her, the most powerful dreams she has, mostly, they run like silent films as dialogue would only mar their pristine beauty, in one, the sky is cast pearl, and they walk along as if on a single breath, on the thinnest line of breath, with the world barely perceptible around them, and they walk along the beach hand in hand, but they could be walking anywhere, they could be floating on an arc of almost becoming, and they are talking, though she can't hear what they're saying, and if she could, she wouldn't remember what they talk about, only that it is about nothing, and that the nothing makes her whole, that the nothing makes her happy, and shells dot the sand, open and empty, some broken, others seemingly intact, more abandoned beginnings or endings, and aren't they the same thing? each existing on the other side of limitlessness, and so she picks one up, shakes out the sand and grime, then runs her finger along the notched rim of transformation, and her life opens wide before her, gaping new, and she imagines the soft bodies that once lived in these places, imagines the stories they held, each holding an infinite number of stories, each story filled with an infinite number of holes, but it is the holes that make them whole, she thinks, and then she wonders if the shell held the soft body together in the same way Julia holds her each night in these dreams, and she understands that love is a shell, and she sits in the sand with Julia, each holding the other's words, feeding them one by one to each other, invisible as longing into a waiting mouth, and occasionally, they spill one and laugh at the poem they've made, and in another dream, she wakes from her bed feeling uneasy, fragile, and she goes to the window of her apartment and finds Julia tending to the lavish English garden that somehow exists where there should be a parking lot, and Julia looks so busy, as if she couldn't wait for the day to begin, as if in rising early she could shape the day into whatever she wanted,  and she is pulling strawberries and eating them as she pulls them, and Allison knows she can go to her, but she decides to stay and watch, to bear witness to this person she loves so, to watch her insatiable desire, how open, how magnificent, and she is content to keep this small secret within her, to guard it with her life, and the red color of strawberries smearing Julia's face is a small gift, and in yet another dream, they sit together outside an LA ice cream shop somewhere in Japan town, and they take turns feeding each other ice cream, and she opens her mouth wide, in part because she can't stop smiling, can't stop laughing at the care and attentiveness with which Julia spoon feeds her, it's as if she's a newborn, and she thinks she could like this, she thinks that every time the ice cream touches her tongue, each time she swallows the cold pineapple flavor, feels it settle deep in her being, it's like taking in an ancient light, and she becomes a vessel of fire, melting it, and she tries to speak, to tell Julia she can't possibly hold anymore, and her voice is like dawn, how delicate, she thinks, how vast the material of dreams, no matter that other life, this world is more real anyway, and so she is content to seek the secret of Julia's face, she is content to look behind what is said, to hear the language of all that cannot be spoken, never mind that she spots that damn mule, Frances, lurking in the corner, hiding in the alleyway beside the ice cream shop, never mind that his brays and laughs threaten to drown the kiss of their silence, well ain't that a horse of a different color, he says, hee-haw, hee-haw, then he stomps his hoof three times, what is dreaming after all but the ebb and flow of something that washes away all we thought we were, hee-haw, hee-haw, and you need a thorough wash, don't you my dear Allison, and though she tries her best to remain in this place where her life is deeper than it is wide, she knows that with each bray, with each stomp of his indelicate hoof, she is moving further and further from this sanctuary of blessed silence, and so she opens her mouth to receive another spoon of ice cream, and so she lets her tongue feel what it is to love, and so when she wakes, it is with a mouthful of birds each carrying the tiniest trace of her desire

# Dream Memory 10

**and** the giant hand extends toward her from the sphere, and the air thrums, and the desert sand vibrates as through a sifter, and in a moment, the desert is no longer what it was, and she is no longer what she was, and how to trace our vanish into such a strong caress? how to know when one being ends and another begins? and how to know when not to fight? we can't blame her for forgetting what it was to kneel in the desert, for forgetting that brief moment when she felt the god inside her, but now she is fighting that god, please remember, Nancy, you have your whole life to be each of yourselves, your whole life to open to the thousand others inside, we know it feels as if they're all fighting to possess you in this brief moment, but it's not true, let them take you, Nancy, let them take you, and remind you again how it feels to walk on your knees, to feel how the giant's hand embraces you, let go, Nancy, and sink deep into that hand and wait for return, wait for the you that will be, feel the fingers' hunger, their calloused tips, an offering, and of course Harry backs away, of course Harry leaves his wife to get his gun from the car, he has always been afraid of the monstrous, not understanding it comes from within, handsome Harry would never look within, better to drown the monster inside with alcohol, with whiskey and bourbon, better to pull out a gun and shoot at the monster outside, and so he shoots at the giant hand, again and again, but still, it keeps coming, reaching for Nancy, reaching for him, silly Harry, why did he think it would be any different, you can't kill a god without or within, and then Nancy cries, Harry, Harry, help me! Harry, help me! but Harry's not made for such violent transformations, he is fashioned from weaker material than his wife, and so he turns tail and runs, and so he climbs in the car and bullets out of there, straight home, leaving her to face the emptiness, to face the sphere, that giant hand, alone, and all she is now is the little comfort we can offer, and so we try as best we can, it's okay, Nancy, we say, the real hero faces the emptiness alone, and that's you, it's certainly not Harry, it's you, it's always been you, because you are known, Nancy, we see you, we are witness to the only act of true heroism a person can do, facing their loneliness, facing the emptiness, and doing it alone, of course it has to be done alone, please don't blame Harry, he simply doesn't have it in him, he lacks the hero's necessary quality, which is, quite simply the ability to be alone in the desert, exactly what you're doing now, because in that place a person can't escape certain thoughts, and you know what they are, the things we never admit to thinking, even in our darkest moments, things like, our love for each other must give way to absence, give way to the unknown, things like how we must jump into the emptiness the same way we might jump into the bark of a tree and let its rings surround us, and of course we must do it in the desert, or perhaps a deep ocean, or maybe a vast blue sky, anywhere that stretches endlessly in the direction of our loneliness, stretches into a perhaps world of becoming, an etching of holy, but still she doesn't believe, perhaps she can't hear us because still she struggles in the giant's grasp, and still she cries to her husband, handsome Harry, Harry, help me! Harry, help me! and so we try once more to make her hear us, we try once more to calm the tide of her fear, as we shout, unwrap the dust from your clothes, Nancy, and spill it over the desert, let the dust that was you drift on the air like a dark river, it is the newly shaped self in the dust you hunger for, feel that hunger, let yourself go and fall into it, take the shape of the hand, and in doing so, you will become the hand, let the hand choose that within you that will then become

and thus the transformation begins, and she is no longer an abstraction watching the film of her life run over and over, and she no longer sits passively in the theatre, nor does she pretend, and she is no longer imitating a life, and she will become enormous, though others may call her monstrous, there is nothing more monstrous than a woman who has become, and she will become eternal, though others may see her death as the only solution, and she has learned the path of rage, and we humans are small and crawl unnoticed, but you, Nancy, you have become a world entire, and then it hits us, and we are overcome, and we wish you were alive, Allison, we wish you hadn't died so early, so tragically, so you could receive the many voices of this book, we wish you'd listened harder to Nancy's struggles instead of writing them off as just another paycheck, just another movie, then you, too, would write the poem that is you becoming desert, becoming dirt, becoming a woman alone hearing the sparrows at dawn, becoming a woman as wanderer over cities and rivers, people, and mountains

# UC San Diego, Medical Center

**and** every person is a reliquary, and Allison is one of the biggest of all, and most of what she holds is grief, but perhaps it is the same for all of us, by the end of a life, we carry so much, there is no container big enough, and yet, we, in our puny bodies must carry it, but maybe we go about it the wrong way, maybe we need to invite it in the house, gesture for it to sit in the kitchen with us where we offer it coffee or tea, because, of course, there is nothing unique to our pain, it is commonplace, like a dog, and there is nothing different about her journey, or ours, her road, our road, is ordained, and she, we, must walk it as a giant, and so, we must turn to Allison and remind her that when things get tough, she must remember it is that way for all of us, and yes, every step will hurt, but those steps will also astonish, and though she no longer walks, not even with her black cane, the biggest step is yet to come, and so Allison lies in bed as two nurses rotate her, they must re-position her every few hours so that she doesn't get bed sores, and they talk as they empty her bladder bag and wipe down her skin, they talk as if she weren't there, which in many ways, she is not, in the ways that matter to this life, she is a vegetable, kept alive by the pinging machines, and so we can't blame these nurses for ignoring her, for thinking her life is over, they have not yet suffered enough to understand that our lives are measured by our hunger, and that hunger doesn't stop just because our bodies do, and so, they prattle on about what they're planning on making for dinner, or what they hope to do this weekend, or how their children made them laugh yesterday, or cry, or how their husbands made them laugh or cry, and when they are done fixing Allison, for that is how they see it, they think they are fixing her, or perhaps arranging her, like a vase of flowers, and after they take one last look at her to admire how they've made something pretty, something they didn't think was there before, something not there already, something not already becoming, they keep talking as they leave her alone again, however, by this point each has ventured a bit too near the truth of their own lives, so they've stopped listening to each other, each retreating into the safe haven of their thoughts, and isn't it interesting how people are so afraid of other people's truths, how they're so terrified, they'll do almost anything to avoid them, which is why Allison prefers the world she's in, with its pinging machines and tubes running into and out of her body because there she's free to dream, she's free to discover a new language, and that new language moves through her like a yawn, it moves through her like a wave, and she knows she's not really speaking it, she knows she's dying, but she sings to the nurses in the new language anyway, because she can tell they need it, and at some level she is happy, oh not happy in the sense that you or I think about it, not happy in the ways that are bought and sold in capitalist America, even the capitalist America of the 1970s, but she is happy nevertheless because she's discovering this new language and because with this new language and in this new space she doesn't have to work as hard to keep hidden the truest parts of herself, she no longer has to worry about accidentally revealing something long kept hidden, and it doesn't matter to her that she only has hours to live, after all, what is time to a person free of the burden of being, a person in process of becoming? and so, at first, she doesn't notice the dark haired, dark eyed middle-aged woman who enters shortly after the nurses leave, and how could she notice, she who no longer sees, who is barely of this world? of course, she could probably still smell her, they say smell is the most primitive sense of all, and it would be the last to go, so perhaps she could smell her, a scent not un-like the creamy caress of late afternoon light over the ocean, but the truth is she feels her presence first, as the air becomes so light she can't breathe it all in, only bit by bit, the same way she must live, day by day, moment by moment, word by word in her new language, and is the woman really there? that's the questions she wants to know, as in truth, she's not sure, it's not like the nurses whose presence was so precise it was unmistakable, and now we understand there are moments that can't be narrated, and that this may be one of those, moments that are beyond what is known, moments that only exist in a difficult light, and so she begins talking, though she doesn't understand how or why, and it's true, if a person only does what she understands, she'll never become, and so she talks in her new language of trees and birds and things incomprehensible to her, and she knows what she says doesn't matter, all that matters is that Julia is there listening, for it is Julia, she's sure of that now, as sure as she can be of anything in this world, which is to say, not terribly sure at all, because so much in this world has a shimmering to it, and at first she thought the shimmering was a distortion, something meant to hide the truth of things, but she's realizing it's not that at all, the shimmering is the strange and difficult light of truth we are not used to seeing, and that's why it shimmers because we spend our whole lives without seeing it, and then suddenly it' everywhere, at least if we are not afraid, if we stand alone in the desert and let the hand take us, if we are willing to become enormous and walk across that desert, so yes, Julia is there listening, and in listening, she tells you the story of your life, and that is the one, true job of listening, isn't it, and yet, how rarely that happens, to have a listener give you such a gift on her knees and in prayer, and so, Allison talks on, and she doesn't need a response, that's not the goal, and Julia knows this, if she's there at all, and the reader knows this, and knows, too, that it doesn't really matter if Julia's there or not, and so the reader says yes, let's pretend she's there because it gives Allison someone to talk to, it gives her an audience, and everyone needs that, especially if that audience is someone you found in a garden, someone who found you, and so, she talks, and she repeats herself, telling the stories of her life, and each time she repeats herself she adds something new, something she didn't know before, and each time she repeats herself she creates the story anew, surprising herself at the twists and turns, the things she'd forgotten and the things that may have never been, and each time she pauses to catch her breath, and perhaps, yes, perhaps listen, too, to see if Julia has anything to say, anything to add, and so she waits, hearing only the sound of the sea, and she confirms to herself each time that she doesn't need a response, the scent of that creamy late afternoon light is enough, the sound of the sea is enough, the naked air and empty space holding them is enough, and she is so happy, so happy in that way we can only begin to understand, we who live in the world of buying and selling, that she doesn't hear the clomp, clomp, clomping of hooves down the hospital hallway, doesn't hear that hee-haw, hee-haw followed by a snickering as the door to her room cracks open

**hand**, hand, hand, palm, fingers, hand as curled fist, hand that wants burning, hand touching, hand extending, hand opening, and Nancy lies in a coma in her bed on the upper floor of her mansion, and no one knows how she returned to the house in this state, only later will the sheriff discover the giant footprints and deduce she was carried back by the aliens, and the only sign that something has happened to her to cause the coma—a few scratch marks around her neck, as if from a fingernail, and the marks glow a strange blue and green color, and she no longer speaks, and of course she'll be voiceless until her transformation, until she rises from her bed as big as a mountain, shouting for her husband, handsome Harry, the philandering husband who wanted to kill her, but now, she is in her cocoon, now she is working through the process of violent transformation, and we are left to watch and wonder, to watch and cry out, O great unknown, we live in terror of you, O guttering candle in the body's final retreat, we cannot imagine, we who witness what can't be told, the transformation of a woman, we live in terror of her limitlessness, yet we hope for it, too, hope for the blessings of her wrath, blessed are those who dare to utter into being, and we wish we could wake one day, like her, without remembrance of the agony of broken, for we are learning, too, but our path is a longer one, we don't know why, some paths are longer, some shorter, that is all, and there is no logic or fairness to it, such is the way of unfolding, and so she sleeps in her bed, unaware of the changes going on inside her, unaware of what she'll become, and meanwhile, her husband, handsome Harry, and his mistress, Honey, sit in the car outside the Archer mansion, her hand caressing his neck as she speaks, there is a way out, if you've got the nerve, she says, the serum that private nurse is using in her hypodermic needle, I heard the doctor telling her an overdose would be fatal, and isn't it strange how events in one world can intrude upon another? strange what we call bad luck or serendipity, chance or fate, strange the seeming coincidences that happen in our daily lives, we don't know what to call them or how to measure them, we only sometimes sense them when the hair stands up on the back of our necks, when we get that odd feeling, and Allison has that odd feeling now when she hears the knock on her apartment door, and she attributes it to the hope she has that somehow the person on the other side will be Julia, though it never is, and how could it be? even in a story where worlds collide as often as they do in this one, that might be a bit much, and this time, it's the delivery man bringing the calcium supplements Allison ordered from England, and she's read somewhere that women are prone to osteoporosis, and her mother suffered horribly from that, and she wants to avoid the same fate, and she's nearly thirty, so she figures there's no time like the present, so she opens the package immediately and takes the prescribed dosage, something she'll do religiously for the next twelve years even when she begins to feel the pain, even when that pain becomes debilitating, in fact, she'll do this until she starts to suspect the pills are poisoning her, but then it will be too late, and Harry returns to the house and sees that the nurse is sleeping, and he takes advantage of the fact to fill the hypodermic to the brim with the serum with which he plans to overdose his wife, and slowly, ever so slowly, he makes his way upstairs, but the nurse isn't sleeping, this nurse is a smart one, she only pretends to sleep, suspecting the dubious Harry of foul play, and so she follows him up the stairs and screams upon entering the bedroom, not because she finds Harry about to plunge the needle into his wife's arm, but because that arm has grown to monstrous proportions because the hand itself is bigger than Harry, and both the nurse and Harry the handsome husband back away in horror, the husband hiding the evidence of his murderous plan as he returns down the stairs, the nurse running to Doctor Cushing who orders chains to hold the giant woman down and an elephant syringe to keep her in the coma until he can figure out what to do because of course he's never seen anything like this, a woman, who, if she grows any bigger, will burst out of her bedroom and through the roof of her own, lavish mansion, and yes he's a doctor, but he can't possibly understand the facts, and the fact is, she's entering a dream, which is the only way truth can come at a person anyway, or rather, the only way a person can live the truth, live through the truth to be more precise, and it is the dream that is shaping her, making her grow, the dream and the hunger for what lies in the dream that are responsible for these changes, and what of we who watch, we who bear witness to this event? is there a chance the dream can shape us, too? a chance for the world to be remade inside us just as it's being remade in Nancy Archer or Allison Hayes? (do you see how little we understand, we don't even know what to call her, as if names were anything more than gauze wrapped around a face), and so let us keep watching and see, but of course objectivity is a dizzying glance, and a difficult one to maintain, so let us not hope for the restrictive lens of objectivity, instead, let's pray we, too, will look with the curved glass of dream, after all, we understand so little of what is happening, of the process of becoming, and that is a point in our favor, after all, up to this point, like Allison, like Nancy, we've done everything we could in order not to see, everything we could not to feel, so, let us watch, for soon she will be losing her chains, and so few people get a chance to slip free from the bonds that bind them, let us watch for soon she'll be scouting the empty possibility in the desert quails scattered through the arroyos, soon she'll be sounding the cadence of cricket and frog-song, more prayer than calling in the cracks in the sediment in the middle of drought, yes, that's right, frog-song in the middle of the desert, yet one more fact in the long line of facts we did not know, frogs and toads, who have been hiding for months, rising out of the desert after rain, as dry washes turn to rivers and sunbaked soils soften and fill with ephemeral water, a complete metamorphosis, of both animal and landscape, punctuated by the bull roar of thousands of frogs, and if a landscape as harsh as the desert can rebuild itself, if an animal as simple as the frog can reconstruct its life, then certainly we, who are so much more, can change, certainly we who build and build until we create our own landscapes, until we transform the very world around us, can overcome the fetters with which we hold ourselves down

# Dream Memory 12

and poison is a stone cast straight at a giant, and there is suffering, and there is disaster, and suffering goes on living, and a thing grows in a woman's body, not a child, but its opposite, a sphere grows in a woman's body, it grows and twists and pinches, it grows and the woman, Allison, begins to think she is going mad, and the next morning, when she opens the door to the shimmering air, the beginning of pain, and it is like a door opening in the sphere that is her stomach, and so with one hand on her belly, the other stretched before her as if she is a blind mendicant, she walks the wearisome road of that pain, as it moves day by day, week by week, month by month, year by year, into her arms, her legs, her head, and she knows this is no dream, this is something more frightening than being chained to a bed, and she can hear her own footsteps as she walks through the pain, then stumbles, or are those steps the clomp, clomping of hooves just outside the door, the door to her pain, she is not sure, and did she buy herself a cane? she can't remember, but she needs one, and she wonders if there was a moment dividing this life from the other? something she could pick out, point to, and the more she thinks, the more she realizes she doesn't know when this door opened, when she walked through, and it feels as if it's been forever, and if she understands one thing, she understands that now she is lost on this road, a road that is starting to feel more like a labyrinth, and her dreams now seem to only be of escape, escape from the labyrinth of this pain, and she thinks how it's funny because she used to tell people she wanted burning, she remembers sitting at a café with friends in those innocent days of youth and saying, I want burning, and by that she meant she wanted to live life fully, to feel everything, including all of its grief, all of its pain, and she remembers being slightly put off when her friends laughed, when they didn't seem to take her seriously, but now she knows how stupid she sounded, now she knows her friends were right, to feel everything deeply, to live everything deeply, now she understands what it means to burn, and no one should wish it on anyone, least of all themselves because it is a curse, and you don't get relief from a curse because a curse is endless, drawing us from one desert to another in the hope that the one who is promised will be waiting there to help us, but there's no one there, except the hand of fire, burning your lips, scorching your tongue, and no matter how many deserts you cross, how many doors you knock on, no one is ever there, and she can't even get the first doctor to do X-rays, she begs and pleads, but all he does is check her heart, tap her stomach, and test her reflexes below the knee, then confidently announce that it's all in her head, and so she tries another, and this time, she at least gets an X-ray, but unfortunately, it will not be the last, there will be three hundred and forty of them over the next twelve years, enough radiation to put down a giant, and like all the X-rays that will follow, this first one shows nothing, and so once again the doctor announces confidently that it's all in her head, all she needs is rest, he says, she is a "high-strung woman," he says, she's been too "worked up" lately, he says, what with the decline in acting offers coming in, all she needs is rest, and so she returns home trying to imagine her way through this new life, wondering what is now left of her, after all, she was on the verge of freeing herself, but what can she do without a body? new planets are discovered so often now that the miraculous feels promised, but a body, you only get one of those, and so she lies in bed day after day, trying to understand what is happening to her only to come to the realization that it's better she escapes the temptation of understanding, that way madness lies, and she's already having difficulty holding on, it was bad enough when the movie offers stopped coming in, bad enough when the pile of bills on her kitchen counter was starting to look like another appliance, and now this, this pain gathering within like a fist, and so she rises from her bed and goes to her piano, trying to find her body again in its music, and she extends her anguished fingers, pushes for Rachmaninov, but fingers falter, and the keys sound incongruous notes, and so she reaches for Chopin, and at first something like a melody comes, but just as quickly it's lost in the pain of her joints, and suddenly, she doesn't know anything anymore, and it's as if all she has left from the dream is pain, and no knowledge of where it comes from, and the sun makes her head hellish, and she closes the curtains and retreats into the darkness, and all we can do is say, poor Allison, she is so in touch with the moment that she doesn't see it, doesn't see that all she needs do is sleep because dreaming is far better than the waking life, because when we dream we are acutely aware of all that is happening, even if we don't understand, but as we've come to know in this life, understanding is vastly overrated

# Dream Memory 13

*Once a normal, voluptuously beautiful woman, now the most grotesque monstrosity of all....Witness the horror! Feel the shock! Experience the frenzy and devastation of the Attack of the Fifty Foot Woman!*

Scene Twenty-One:

Dr Cushing: "I've known Nancy since she was born." He puffs on his pipe as he paces in the garden. "In those days, she was a beautiful child. Fresh. Young. Full of the joys of life." He is talking to his colleague, Dr. Heinrich Von Loeb, who is seated at the edge of a fountain, smoking a cigarette. "But in the last few years, after her marriage, she changed. Her health seemed to rise and fall with the tide of her emotions."

Dr. Von Loeb: "A very sad case. A case not infrequent in this supersonic age we live in."

Scene Twenty-Two:

Nancy: "Harry. Harry. Harry. I want out of here," she yells for her husband, handsome

Harry, as she wakes.

Doctor Cushing: "Nurse, hurry with that morphine." Both doctors rush upstairs along with the nurse.

Nurse: "She's loose. She'll tear the roof off."

Voice of Nancy: "I know where my husband is. He's with that woman." Her voice echoes through the house. Her hands are curled into fists as she punches her way through the roof, rafters raining down on the doctors, the nurse. With each passing second, there is a little less moon in the sky, and as she rages, and as the doctors run, a bee orbits an unknowable flower. As she screams and tears down what remains of her home, a lone bee ignores the cascading beams and rafters.

and now she becomes first no longer no longer still no longer and still endlessly suddenly finally still sphere looming sphere watching making a breadcrumb path she rises up up up into sky tree growing smaller roads shrinking below first the world is one way then it is not and she tries to put it back never mind the broken ignore the smashed and crumpled houses at her feet anywhere a person can go anywhere no need to return it no need and where does she want to go I know where my husband is he's with that woman is that what she wants and so she stands above the ruins of her home for a long time thinking thinking thinking

what becomes of the past if the future snaps the pain's the
same the pain's a sphere growing inside her making her
enormous now she breathes in the clouds and sees it whole
every desolation and loneliness every sorrow and suffering
she's traveling beyond her story traveling far beyond her
story up into clouds up into divine was it God's wounded
hand reaching out to her scratching her neck placing the
sphere inside an egg of pain of knowledge of grief an eye of
understanding inside the egg a giant inside the eye a giant
rising into sky and then it is quiet in her mind and what is
she seeing but the curve of everything joining everything
else and she is growing outside the world the beautiful
child fresh young full of the joys of life is now an enormous
thing outside of pity or love and everything is bursting with
silence with the scent of desert sand with the trail laid out
before her and it's there beneath the truth of stars and she's
finally she's endlessly beginning she's not ashamed hunger
she's endlessly hungry not ashamed each woman her own
chance at hunger and people must see people must see her
and the rocks are humming a long steady drone and she
walks across the shining desert alone and she walks among
the stones stooping picking them like marbles to play and
her other hand opens scratched and raw fluttering like a
strange bird like a wild flower reaching reaching reaching

Scene Twenty-Three:


Dr. Cushing: Taking the pipe from his mouth, his back to his friend, who is still seated on the edge of the fountain. "I'm afraid I was unwise in advising her to take Harry back after they'd separated."

Dr. Von Loeb: Standing, walking toward Dr. Cushing. "Who knows my friend. When women reach the age of maturity, Mother Nature sometimes overworks their frustration to a point of irrationalism."

and houses are snapping and shadows rise like hills above the earth and now they run the shadows of this story the sheriff and his deputy chase after in pursuit and the Doctors follow too more shadows shadows upon shadows and of course her husband handsome Harry all of them shouting words like prayers words a kind of nonsense and they will not let her be alone a giant in the world and they will not let her be non-existent in a giant world and they will not let her be giant in a non-existent world

awaken dearest Allison
awaken dearest Nancy
awaken

**and** her pain is a dark room, and that dark room exists inside the sphere, the enormous white sphere from her last failed movie, *Attack of the Fifty-Foot Woman,* and so she stands in the middle of the room inside the sphere, feeling along the walls for a light switch, and we know the scene because we've been there, too, many times, so many times, and we will be there again, and so we can't help but wonder what might happen if we were free to accept or refuse the pain, free to have a choice, but who would make such a choice? there are always those who willingly or not undertake great destinies, people who move through life with stubborn pride, uncomprehendingly, but she is not one of them, nor, to be honest, are we, and our poor, dear Allison, or Nancy, or whatever you want to call her by this point, is afraid, for she had no idea the pain would be this bad, the pain is too much, if she tries to get up from her bed, her legs will give way before she finds the light switch, and she'll crumple and fall to the floor, alone, and no one will ever find her, and she'll lie there for days, perhaps weeks, and no one will come by, and she'll die there, alone, and when they find the body, it will be because of the smell, she's sure of this, she's seen it in her mind's eye many times, women always die on a bare floor, she thinks, no matter what they do, no matter how they lived their life, and she knows, too, that even if she finds the switch, her hands will stiffen and curl into claws or her arms will become leaden, and she won't be able to flip it, worse still is something she doesn't dare tell herself or even think, except in her darkest moments, and then she banishes the thought away, out beyond the sphere, out beyond the room, and that thought is this—what if she manages to find the light switch and turn it on, but there is no light? what if the switch doesn't work, and she remains in darkness, what if the darkness is all she has, and her job, her lesson in life, is to learn to cherish it, to cherish that darkness, but who could do that? and of course, you can never really banish a thought like that, and even if you do, it comes right back, it stays with you, waiting, like a patient cat, ready to pounce on its prey when that prey is most vulnerable, and so she spends whole hours sometimes, lying in the dark on either the bed or the floor, lying there, thick in her disbelief, but praying, always praying, and looking toward her window, praying for some kind of light, hoping that God will be there, or perhaps a bird, a sparrow, looking back at her, and occasionally, she finds herself, for a moment, outside the room, or rather, she carries the room with her when she manages to find the strength, which is not often, but when she does find the strength to carry the room with her, to carry the sphere with her, she visits a new doctor and gets more X-rays done, and again, she's told that it's all in her head, the dark room of pain is in her head, you have to be patient, a voice says in the darkness, and she doesn't know whether it's the doctor's or a bird's, sometimes the night is long, the voice says, sometimes the night is oh so long and you have to be patient, and then she's sure the voice sounds like that of a bird, a little bird like a sparrow or a chickadee, it's high and melodic, and sometimes it chirps at her, and this place can't be all bad, she thinks, if there is a bird here, too, but what if the bird is trapped as well? what if it's a prison for it, too? what if it, too, is seeking the light, looking for a window, and that's its failing, and that's why it is lost in here, too? are you trapped in this room, as well? she asks, I'll find a way out, don't worry, but trust me, the way out is not through the window, that's a trick, and her thinking echoes inside the room inside the sphere, and she tries to rid herself of the echoes by pulling at her hair and finds that her hair comes off in clumps, is it because of the X-rays? and she pulls at her hair, and clump after clump comes out, and she can't see it, but she feels the handfuls of hair, and she decides to make a nest for the bird, that's the way, she thinks, if it can't get out at least it can have a home, you're simply distracting yourself, the bird says, you're avoiding your pain by focusing on mine, and she covers her ears so she won't have to hear the bird but soon realizes that she can't live without the bird, she can't live alone with the pain, it's too much, and she wishes she could see the bird, but since she can't, she must at least hear it, and it's then the bird tells her to build another room, if you can't live in this one, build another, it's what I do, the bird says, I have many rooms inside me, and so, she constructs another room in her dreams, a room in which she doesn't suffer from this pain that emanates from her center and spreads through her body like a wave, a continuous wave, and it's a small room with a little light, but at least it's enough to see by, and she can sit there with a good book and read the day away, and the bird is a sparrow, and it has accepted the nest of her hair, and it sits in the nest atop the tree lamp in the corner of her newly built room, speaking to her, this is a good room, it says, it reduces your pain to a manageable size so you can go out and do things, it says, and she hasn't thought of that, she only thinks of this new room as a pillow stuffed in her mouth so that she can't hear her own screaming, she didn't think of this room as a way of moving in the world, and perhaps the sparrow is right, and she asks the sparrow if it has a name, but it doesn't answer, it seems it only talks when it wants to talk, and so, she takes her room out with her to meet her agent, to see if she can get work, as she needs work if she's going to pay all the doctor bills piling up on her desk, for there is a desk with bills on it in the room, too, every room must have that, even a dark little room inside a sphere, inside a body, but her agent tells her that no one wants to work with her, her agent says that she's earned a reputation, and she thinks that "earned" is a strange choice of words and tells him so, but he tells her that people say she's crazy, that she sees things, that she talks to people who aren't there, and she tells her agent that she's simply talking to her pain, and he says, that's it, right there, that's what I'm talking about, who says things like that? and he tells her he can do nothing for her until she gets hold of herself, and she tells him that he is the darkness, she says that she thought she escaped the darkness, but he is it, other people are it, the world is it, and nothing is lost to the darkness, she says, nothing is lost because it's all here within me, within the room, within the sphere, and she goes home and dyes what remains of her hair black, circles her eyes with blue moons, and she tells the sparrow to peck out what remains of her eyes so she can see deep into the corners of the little room she has built, and that's when she hears the other voice, the one she's tried to forget so many times, a horse once told me that any attempt to live in the darkness is an illusion, the voice says, hee-haw, hee-haw, and then the hoof stomping three times, and she tells Frances to shut up, she tells him he has no right to enter this room she has built, and he says, you think this room you built is small, but I tell you it is vast, I tell you it contains everything, so how could I not be here with you, and then he stomps his hoof three times and lets out a bray so big it sounds like a laugh

# Dream Memory 15

once once once in a dream a woman in a dream a woman growing growing becoming mystery becoming monster changing into forever forever forming transforming shaking grief shaking contrition pain breaking break through earth break stone break the back of this faithless world and she glows like the moon like a giant white sphere and she radiates her mortal flesh lit from within now lit by her pain a fire of pain a white fire freeing her from this world burning everything and she is returning to the sky walking her way into days into weeks into the divine and she knows this because she knows hunger again and knowing hunger she reaches for God and the moon forever rising and setting and the moon forever she is the moon rising she is a giant sphere revealing itself in the desert a mountain moving across the desert police and doctors in pursuit and no matter they'll never catch her they can only hear the rivers that flow from her they can only dream of lying in the meadows she leaves behind they cannot know her geology it is continually transforming she is today what she will be tomorrow what she has always been and so she must learn to walk then to dance slowly across the world and it is new to her this world this walk this dance and once she remembers practicing years ago as a child then forgetting in the blindness of adulthood and she dances always ahead of them the police the doctors the directors and producers and she dances always over them over their offices their movie studios and she hurls rafters and splintered roof upon them and she walks over rivers and streams no longer needing to drink for they flow from her and she walks only with hunger Harry she says the name of her husband handsome Harry and knows she no longer cares for him no longer cares about him and she doesn't want him doesn't love him doesn't hunger for him and her hunger is for something else her hunger is all she is now and it is everything and once she loved a man named Harry and then she stopped end of story and it's time for a new story and she's grown beyond the shit show beyond the politicians and the producers beyond the movies and TV ads telling you what to buy beyond the culture of distraction and she's grown beyond the wars the bombs and their endless killing beyond the greedy streets darkening with flies beyond the silly skyscrapers so obviously phallic beyond the need for phallic and the table is cleared of her place and she is free to start again and she turns from the dishes in the sink she turns from the basket of laundry and sees the little room from which she came the dark room within which she made her own even smaller room with a sparrow for company and she takes the little room in her enormous hand and she carries it with her always and when she is ready she will make a nest for it inside her and she will gently oh so gently place the room there on a bed of leaves a delicate bed of leaves to protect it, and we are the moon she says we are the hand of five stars we are the mountain and the river once once once in a dream a woman in a dream her hand reaches toward the fire now but it doesn't burn and for those watching her walk for the lonely and drunk miner for the teenage couple making out in the car for the married couple and the businessmen running in the street they see but they don't see they can't really see not exactly her body only her walk only her movement and the spirit of her body a shining a shining in the darkness a white spirit shining and they can't look at her for long for she is too bright as if she glows from radiation and she glows as if she's touched silence she glows as if she's sat for long hours deep in the darkness, so long in the darkness that she's made her own light, that she's become her own guttering candle and now she glows as if she's touched the hand of God and the drunk miner and the teenage couple making out in the car and the married couple and the businessman running in the street see her but can't really see her and so they follow because they hunger for that too because they hunger for whatever makes her shine too even though they don't know that they

do even though if you or I were to ask them why they follow
why they look up at her they would answer that they don't
understand why that perhaps it's because they are terrified
but terror is also attraction for what we most fear for what
we most want and when they look upon her they can almost
touch it too

**and** so she's already a ghost when she appears on *Gomer Pyle U.S.M.C.* as the love interest of Sergeant Carter, she's already long gone into the dark room of her pain, but you wouldn't know it by looking at her, she's still beautiful in that skimpy black dress and those long legs, that 36-23-36 inch figure, and Sergeant Carter makes his move on her in the diner, and just as he's about to kiss her, Private Pyle calls to tell him something urgent about his trip to Washington D.C., rinse and repeat, that's the plot, and next time she's in an orange dress at a bar with the Sergeant, and later an elegant zebra skin affair as they chat in the lobby, and she's found a way to temporarily shut out the dark room, to smile and pretend everything is normal, and remember it's not hard for a woman to do, they're trained from a young age to smile, to not complain, to make the men around them feel good, and she does it better than most, and Sergeant Carter is feeling extra fine today, but she, well, she's far from normal, and what keeps her sane is focusing on the fact that after the shoot she's going to stop by Julia's, something she's never done before, in fact, she hasn't contacted Julia since they worked together all those years ago, as she's afraid that if she did, Julia would make an excuse, would find a way to leave her, to not talk to her, and so she decided a couple weeks ago she would do it, she would tell Julia of her undying love, how she dreams of her every night, how she longs again for the moment in the garden, because a woman can peer into a faraway window, but she can only imagine the life inside, and she's tired of imagining, and so she's sleuthed around until she found the address, and she's decided it will be today, but first she needs to pay those bills, and so she smiles for Sergeant Carter and bats her eyes, and next week it will be *The Guiding Light,* something else after, as long as she gets paid, it doesn't matter what, and don't we move so swiftly through our lives, she thinks, don't we spend most of our time smiling and batting our eyes to pay the bills, to pay for the doctors we see to desperately keep us alive so that we can then wake up each day only to smile and bat our eyes at the Sergeant Carters of the world, an endless circle, the mountain always hidden behind the clouds, well, perhaps, not always, sometimes we get a glimpse, a glimpse of a woman in white in a garden where every flower is a mercy, a woman with dark hair and dark eyes, and that glimpse is enough to last decades, to last our whole lives even, and now she sees a girl in braids sitting in the corner, waiting patiently for the shoot to end, the daughter of one of the crew she guesses, and this girl looks bored, as if she'd rather be anywhere else, and so during the break, she approaches the girl and says to her, a mountain is moving across the dark land, moving toward you with a force you won't understand, and what it brings you won't know until it crashes into you, until you're the mountain, and she doesn't know why she says this, but the girl looks at her as if she's crazy, then gets up and walks toward her father, one of the cameramen as it turns out, don't be afraid, she says to the girl as she walks away, don't . . . and then, as if the words unleashed the pain, it comes in a great wave from the center of her to wash across her body, as if it lay waiting for her to let down her guard again, and she must leave the studio, and she tells the director she can't continue, she can't possibly continue, she doesn't mention the dark room, though she's sure he can see it inside her, how can he not? it has become enormous, the room consumes her, and he must think she's a monster, a monster rampaging through town, you've got a contract, the director says, you can't just leave whenever you want, but she flees the set anyway, the director shouting for her to return, repeating himself, you've got a contract, and she's gone, driving like a maniac on her way to Julia, afraid she won't make it before she loses herself again, but when she gets there, she stops half a block away and parks at the curb, and she stays in her car, unable to will her legs to move, it's not the pain, she thinks, though the pain is crippling, the pain could stop an army, it's simply that she's afraid, what if Julia opens the door and denies her? what if she denies that the night in the garden even occurred? what if when she goes to peer through the window, the window in that dark room, what if when she goes to open it, that window opens to another window, what then? and her blood buzzes in her head until she can't think any more, until she passes out in the seat, and when she wakes, it is in her car at the edge of a great wood, and she runs screaming into the woods, searching for its black heart, and the branches cut at her as she runs, and then, quite unexpectedly, she stops, knowing she is where she needs to be, and there is Julia standing in the middle of the wood, standing across from her, beckoning to her, and she joins her, and they walk hand in hand, and the woods are dark, there is darkness all around them in fact, but she's no longer afraid because Julia is with her, and that's all that matters, and they talk for hours about everything and nothing as they stroll through the woods, and she raises a hand to her mouth in an attempt to measure her life, and she feels the contours and realizes she's smiling, it's not my face, she thinks, this cannot be my face, who am I? she asks Julia, we are not what we think we are, Julia replies, and she understands, the moment we are born we invent the thing we think we are, but we are not that, and then the world tells us we are something else, sometimes it's the thing we invented, sometimes it's at odds with that thing, and no matter what, in the end, the world wins, that doesn't matter, Julia says, what matters is what we are now, at this moment, in these woods, and it's true, it's so true, at first, Allison thinks she'll go mad with the revelation, she doesn't want it, it's too much for her, but then bit by bit the darkness calms her, bit by bit, the feel of Julia's hand in hers calms her, and they enter a meadow filled with wildflowers and stop walking, and Julia turns to her and holds her face in her hands, you're losing yourself, she tells her, the pain is consuming you, you need a plan, but Allison isn't listening, she's thinking only that she wants to die, to die right here in Julia's arms in the middle of the woods, she's thinking that animals are agents of the divine, she's thinking that animals don't distinguish between dreaming and waking, and that she is now an animal, you need to have the calcium pills tested, Julia goes on, breaking her reverie, have them tested because I think they are poisoning you, and a soft wind haunts the leaves, a soft wind like a sigh, like dark hair in the mirror, a soft wind like the tenderness of a dog, and Allison wakes on her living room sofa, and how she got here she doesn't know, and so she rises and goes to the mirror in the bathroom, and she stares at herself there, how can I know? she thinks, the noises of the world have been buzzing at her for so long that they've all become one single noise buzzing in her head, buzzing in the middle of the dark room, how can I know? she thinks again, how can I know anything with all this buzzing? and then she sees a vision of herself bigger than a mountain, bigger than the pain inside her, she sees a vision of herself striding across a desert, glowing like the desert, and she speaks to the mirror, if I tell you my dreams, is it enough? will it be enough? to stem the tide of pain, and the mirror does not answer back

# Dream Memory 17

**as** I've come to see it, I have three options, one—commit suicide, two—go to a psychiatrist in an attempt to live with the pain, accepting the fact that doctors can't diagnose it, and three—find answers myself, and so she stops writing in her journal, puts down the pen, and she is alone in her room, the white walls and ceiling, the stained wood floor holding her, acting as counterpressure to the growing sphere inside, the sphere pushing at the limits of the dark room of her body, and she reaches for a glass of water to free her, then heads to the library, and there days pass as she checks out book after book, and she is amazed to discover the mystery that there is anything at all beyond the dark room, she's forgotten there are clouds, trees, cars, other people, and she finds a book called *Toxicology of Industrial Metals* and reads about factory workers whose symptoms are eerily similar to her own, it seems they'd been exposed to high amounts of lead, breathe, she tells herself, breathe, she takes notes but has long since lost the use of her right arm, so she must take the notes with her left, but her handwriting looks like that of a child, she feels like a child for the first time in forever because she can barely control her excitement, her excitement is like a sparrow aflutter in her ribs, it's like a giant shining over the desert landscape, a blossoming giant, and she returns home and lies awake all night in the darkness, and lying there she fills the entire room, she fills the air, and filled with her, the air is heavy like an embrace, and she's sure that it will rain, and if it rains, then she can sleep, but it does not rain, and so she rises, takes her cane and hobbles to the kitchen because she's certain the answer is here, somewhere, she feels it because everything a person fails to see during the day, at night is revealed, and that's why they must sleep, why we must sleep because we can't stand the revelation, and that's also why we don't sleep because we can only handle so much revelation., better to toss and turn all night, better to move groggily through the morning, then bear the sight of it, but she is beyond sight now, she's deep in the realm of martyrs, of seers and mendicants, for she's long held more than a passing knowledge of hell, and she understands that everything we know is hidden only because we refuse to see, and that's when she spies the calcium pills and vitamins on the table, the pills she's been taking as long as she's had the pain, and the shadows about her swirl into a picture she understands, and the answer she's been searching for has been right in front of her all along, and so she pulls out the phone book and looks for chemists, toxicologists, whoever might be able to confirm what she already knows to be true, and she circles three and calls them the next day, and when she's done, when she hangs up the phone, she says, I love you, and she ventures to say it again but catches herself, to whom is she saying this? she's not sure, was it to Julia? she thinks, was it to herself? or was it to the darkness? perhaps it was her way of surrendering to that world, of saying I accept you, but you will not control all of me, she thinks, I am wilder than that, more complex, more complete, and two weeks later she gets a call from the toxicologist, one hundred and ninety parts per million of lead in each of her calcium pills, each and every one, and he is an older gentleman who cautions her not to be alarmed by the results, he tells her that the government doesn't regulate lead, and doesn't understand all the effects of it, but that this is probably too much, he tells her she shouldn't worry, that it's probably not affecting her at all, but then again, he says, the level does seem quite high for such a little pill, and she stands there in wonder staring at the phone on the wall, and thinks I've opened the door now, I've really opened the door, and she has, she's opened the door and seen Bluebeard's wives, and now what will she do, what will she ever do now that she's looked inside, for if she talks, he will certainly come after her with his knives, with his large hands, and he will undoubtedly try to kill her, to lock her in the room with the other bloody corpses, and she wonders about all the women who discovered the truth in the past, so many women, and yet she's never thought about them before, and why should she have? all of them locked away like that, locked away so they can't speak? no, she thinks, they're already dead, their tongues silenced forever, they are locked away so no one sees what happens to a woman who discovers the truth, no one sees what can become of that kind of woman, and again she wonders what she will do, she could close the door, she thinks, close it and walk away, pretend not to know, or, she could open it wider, she can open it so wide it will be impossible for people not to see, and in doing so, she'll become monstrous, people will see her as a monster, she'll become a giant, a monstrous giant, but for those women, she'll storm like a giant, like a god, through town and make sure everyone hears her thunder, yes, that's what she can do, and so she hobbles to her desk, takes the pen up in her left hand and addresses the first letter to the government of the United States, the second will go to the company in England that makes the pills, and the third will go to her lawyer, it's a good thing she has a lawyer, a good thing she tried to sue the studio and Jack Palance all those years ago, a lawyer will come in handy now, and as she writes, she hears the locusts buzzing through the open window, and their noise is enormous

# Dream Memory 18

she can't stop now that she's started it because it feels too good to pick cars from the road and toss them like toys, to knock over buildings with a wave of her hand, there's no going back, she thinks, no going back to the way things were, no going back to lying in bed all day in a dark room, no way, the buildings, the houses, the cars were built so carelessly, doesn't anyone understand how easy it is to knock it all down, to destroy the illusion that any of it has meaning, destroy the myth that all of this building, building, building will keep the door to the dark room closed, that it will keep Bluebeard's wives locked and shut, the threads of diligent spiders, that's all they are, all these buildings, but she doesn't want to think any more, thinking leads to building and building leads to blindness, and so she leaves the work to her hands, she trusts her hands, o but dear Nancy, even hands can betray, you must understand that, hands are still a part of us, and we cannot be trusted, therefore, they can't be trusted, they feel our sadness and rage, most of all they feel our hunger, it has always been this way, so don't be fooled by the idea that hands will lead you, that hands will act always on good faith, they plot and scheme, too, and that's when she spies the speakeasy where she knows her husband takes that floozy, what's her name? Honey? yes, isn't it the perfect name for another of Bluebeard's wives, a name that invites sex, another distraction, another building, another thread, all that mindless grabbing and rubbing, poor Harry, thinking he's choosing Honey when he's not choosing anything at all, he's simply following the thoughtless clatter of hunger, well, she'll destroy that, too, and in an instant, the door to the dark room closes, she's no longer interested in keeping it open, much less opening it further, in an instant, her pain is back, even though she's a giant, a god, and thought she was beyond pain, are we ever, really, beyond pain? the answer is no, the answer is that the journey ends when we become people bending down, searching for pieces we have owned, pieces we used to build our lives, pieces we now want to destroy, and it's so easy ripping off the rafters, almost too easy, and that's when she thinks of that monster she'd read about in high school,  Grendel, no Grendel's mother, even more monstrous because she's a woman, because she hungers, because her mayhem and rage is not mindless, but precise, the precision of her desire to do harm to the world of men, the way she simply touched the great, oak door to the mead hall, and it burst into splinters, that's what she feels like now as she rips the roof of the speakeasy away, splinters raining down on all those screaming people inside, people who just moments ago thought they were actually choosing something, actually deciding to dance, to kiss, to grope, when all they were really choosing was to avoid the dark room, to refuse Bluebeard's key, that's the moral of that fairy tale isn't, don't look too closely, don't ask too many questions, especially if you're a woman, and she wonders then if there was ever a woman strong enough to take the key but not open that door, what might that woman be like, what might that woman become, a woman who can hold the lie within her, not her, that's all she knows, not her, and so she reaches her hand inside the speakeasy, and the deputy sheriff pulls his gun but can't bring himself to "shoot a lady," so, Harry takes the gun and shoots instead, such a gentleman, her husband, handsome Harry, more like a fly, a fly buzzing, and now the people inside will scream, now they will have reason to scream, and then silence as they see her giant head rise above them like a sun, a silence filled with flies, flies shining black as if born from a dark room, a dark sun, as if they are the very air of that room come to life, and then she spies her husband, and her husband spies her, like addicts who recognize each other on the street, and almost as an afterthought, she sees Honey ducking under a table, as if that will protect her, and then her hand acts, the action surprises her, as if she didn't understand her hand could have a will of its own, a hunger of its own, as if she didn't know a hand can betray a body like that, and her hand peels a particularly large beam from the roof and hurls it at the table, at Honey, smashing her beneath, and Harry runs to Honey, holding her in his arms as if he loves her, and now the sparrow has moved from the dark room inside her to her head, it's flown straight up into her ear, o Nancy, what are you supposed to do with the little bird that sings in your ear? the sparrow that sings, telling you it is enough, it's never enough, is it, Nancy? never enough, and what dark thing is it that we need? what greedy thing is this existence that makes a hand throw giant beams, that makes a hand grasp like a claw? Harry, Harry, she screams, and there are ways of grasping we haven't yet divined, levels of pain we can always descend to no matter how bad we think it is now, and her hand reaches toward Harry, and she knows him in her deepest skin, no, no, Nancy, no! Harry screams, and she knows him, as she knows herself, and she does not like what she sees, no, Nancy, no, you killed Honey! and she grabs him but still he keeps saying it, no, Nancy, no, you killed Honey, put me down, Nancy, I can't breathe, and her hand now the only god, her hand now the only thing that exists outside the dream, and what is dreaming after all but the rise and fall of something that comes to wash away all we are, and, in doing so, promises what? that perhaps we might sidle out of darkness into light

# Dream Memory 19

**and** she has started walking again without the cane, and the pain diminishing like a phantom shuddering out of focus, and the sphere diminishing, too, and she lives now in the space of the door, opening and shutting, opening and shutting, and each week she writes another letter to the government trying to get action, to get someone to listen, to acknowledge her, and each day she waits at her mailbox, but no return letter arrives, and so she does more research and discovers the same lead is being put in baby food, more bodies locked away in the room, and she needs to tell someone, she wants to see the doctors who told her she was neurotic, she wants to tell them they were wrong, but she's so tired, why is she always tired? and now she's developed a rash, and is it always hot in the dark room? the door is open now, she can walk without the cane, the pain has diminished, it should be cooler, so why is she always hot? and why can't she sleep at night? she wants to leave the dark room, but she is afraid she's been there too long, she's afraid her body only remembers the dark, and that's why it's so hot, why she has this rash, why she can't sleep, and so she begins looking out that open door, wondering what it might be like to step outside, to gaze at the flat moon, pale and raw, and she goes to the sink, cups water to her face, maybe that will cool her, and she opens the nearly barren fridge and removes a bowl of stale rice, maybe it's all the strength she needs, and she leaves the cane by the front door, and hobbles down the steps to the street where her car sits, this doesn't mean I'm good, she thinks, I've never done anything to help anyone, this doesn't mean I'm good, but they must know the truth, and I am the only one who can speak it, but it doesn't mean I'm a saint, or a god, Christ, just look at me, I can barely make it to my car, she thinks, I don't even know if I can drive, I'm not equipped to cross the desert, alone, and still, her chest aches with joy, still, she will tell the truth, and they must listen to her, if the government won't answer, she'll make the doctors listen, she'll make the lawyers listen, and she'll start with what's his name? Doctor Cox? he called her neurotic, the last time she went to his office, well, she'll show him, and now she's driving across the bottom of the ocean floor on the way to the doctor's, and where have all the buildings gone? she wonders, where are the people? only water, so much water rising, she could drown in it, but she won't let herself, and she must see the doctor, she must tell the truth, I'm alive, she says to the doctor by way of introduction, there's little left of me, but what's there is finally alive, you have a lymphoma, Allison, he replies, why does he answer as if he hasn't heard?

she says it again, I'm alive, and there is a thing that shines in me, something in the darkness inside me that glows, I need you to understand this, and in answer, he says again, Allison, you have a lymphoma, we've been trying to reach you, but you haven't answered your phone, he says your test results came back positive, I'm afraid it's quite advanced, and then she wonders, what is she if she tells the truth but is not heard? what is she? she wants to know, but she waits and finds no answer, how can there be an answer, she's opened the door and stepped out of the room and yet still no one can hear her, I'm not going back, she says, I'm not closing the door, now that I have the key I won't keep it secret, do you hear me? she says, but the doctor turns to welcome his next patient, and there is a thing in me, she repeats, something that glows in the dark room, and it is a shining in the darkness, so it can't be bad, and now it's in me, and I want to know what to do with this thing because sometimes it shines so bright that I can't see, and it's almost like I looked too deeply and too long, and then she hears the next patient, clomping in on all four legs, Frances, the Talking Mule, of course it is, and she thinks she can escape the dark room, but she can't escape him, he won't leave her alone, not ever, don't pay attention to her, Doc, Frances says, she's neurotic, there's nothing inside her but rot, and the doctor laughs, I read the tabloids, the doctor says, one hundred bathing suits in her closet, a new car each week, a new swimming pool each month, and Frances pounds the floor with his right, front hoof five times, you don't say, the doctor says, really? she dates five men at the same time, she's a real floozy that one, a real man killer, shut up! she tells Frances, shut up and go away! why are you always following me? why are you here? but Frances doesn't budge an inch, he just hits the ground with his hoof three more times, you know why he's here, the doctor says, because nobody can ask for more than someone else can give, and you ask for so much, I'm only asking to be heard, she screams, but that's too, too much, the doctor says, and Frances rears his mule head back and brays his mule bray, hee-haw, hee-haw, and nobody makes up something that doesn't exist, Frances says, I'm here because you want me here, because you're afraid, so afraid, and you need me to keep that hunger in check, so don't be the kind of woman who breaks whatever she touches, go home to the pasture and chew on that hay, and she stands for a moment with a ragged gaze, and it no longer hurts her that the doctor doesn't understand, because she knew she had to speak, she has to speak, still, and she spoke, and she will continue to speak, whether they understand or not is of no importance to her anymore, a woman eventually must speak, and now she has spoken, she's told nearly everyone, she took the key and opened the door, and now the door is open, she's done that, and if people dare to look inside, it's up to them, and if they shut the door, it won't stay locked now, she has spoken and broken the lock, she has spoken, and it can never be locked again, and so she smiles at Frances, and though he pretends not to see it, pretends to be fascinated with the flies orbiting his own behind, she knows he does, and he doesn't like it, not one bit, and she retreats to her apartment, to the dark room, but she's not going in the dark room, not again, not ever again, and so she puts on a clean, ironed nightgown, then combs her hair, and by these small acts she returns to the habits by which she might recognize herself, she's been touched by the hand of god, she knows this now, that's why she's lived so long in the dark room, but now she's opened the door, she did that, and now it can't be locked again, but there's one more thing she must do, and she's a little afraid because already the fight has taken so much from her, her friends, her hair, her sight, yes, she can barely see now, barely make out the road through the desert, and she knows that road will not be an easy one, so yes, she's a little afraid, maybe more than a little, but that's okay, she thinks, that's okay, flowers always panic before they blossom

**and** so let us dive with her to the desert floor where what is imagined is true, let us see the Cactus Wren, the Burrowing Owl, see the Sidewinder and Jackrabbit, let us watch her rise up with sand in her hair, arms armored with the quills of cacti, and what is this drowning we do? willing ourselves into the desert air or into another consciousness, what is this thing we do as we watch her walk, watch her rage beyond the bridle of any dream? she's got Harry! she's got Harry! the town screams, put him down, Mrs Archer! oh the richness of getting old, of being a woman over forty, who do they call Mrs Archer? a woman over forty isn't she herself, she is someone else, someone else entire, and now she's walking toward the thought that every person must have once in their lives, she's walking across the desert toward the thought, and the townspeople are shooting at her, and they are calling the name of Mrs. Archer, but who is that person? she no longer knows, and she's walking toward the thought and away from that person, and she's walking through the desert, and what will she do with the desert? what will she do with the buried horizon? the desert is eternal, and the body teaches us only to be mortal, but she is no longer the body, she is the sphere,

she is the horizon and she is the light in the dark room, she
is a shining in the darkness, and she is made of sparrows,
and she's flying quickly across the desert, she's flying toward
the thought, or perhaps she is the thought, and that is why
the guns don't hurt her, that is why bullets pass through
her, because she is the thought, because she is made of fire
and light, and still, it is not enough, and still she hungers
for more, she wants burning, she wants to teach the body
now what it means to be immortal, she's got Harry! she's got
Harry! the town screams again, put him down, Mrs Archer!
and the fact that they don't understand her, don't know her
true name, no longer matters because she understands them,
and she understands that understanding is a way of looking,
that understanding is always there in front of you, it is a
matter of choice, and she's made her choice, she's chosen
the thought, and then she sees it rising out of the desert, the
tower with the power lines, standing alone in the desert the
way she's stood alone all her life, the power lines call to her
because they, too, are made of thought, made of light, and
that light calls to her, the light in the dark that helps her see
things, see the things with false names, calls to her, and the
sparrows in her fly toward it, and then she's there, her light
stands beside its light, stands within its light, and now she
no longer wants to be anywhere else, and now she no longer
hungers, no longer needs to fly, she only needs the eternity

of this light, the light inside her, and the light outside, and so she stands beside the tower with the power lines for a lifetime, two lifetimes, and she doesn't care that the sheriff has gone back to the station, back to his gun cabinet to find his biggest gun, she doesn't care about the townspeople running toward her, shouting the name of a person she used to know, a person she can only faintly remember if at all, she's no longer part of that world, if she ever was, and now the thought frees her, the thought she has become frees the last sparrow within her, and as it flies out of the dark room, it knocks the door off its hinges, the thought frees the last sparrow within her, and when it flies off, the sphere hovering always within the room that is her crashes to the floor, and her grief shatters in a thousand tiny shards, and she reaches out her hand, she stretches her hand toward the powerlines, she reaches for the light, and now she no longer sees the townspeople, no longer sees their shouting faces, no longer understands their hunger, for she is beyond that, she is beyond the game, the game of pretending, the game of pretending you don't know, the game of building things and pretending, the game of taking the key and pretending you aren't going to look in the room, but everyone knows, everyone has looked in the room at one point or another, everyone has always known, they just pretend not to, and now she knows, and that's all that matters, others before her have tried to break the silence, and now she has, she's broken everything, and now she's walked across the desert, and no one can stop her, and now she can reach toward the thought, she can hold the thought, and the sheriff raises his big gun, and she reaches out her hand, and he shoots his big gun, and she reaches toward the thought, the thought that is everything, and she's losing the ability to speak, losing the ability to exist in words, but that's okay, she only has this one last thing to do, she exists only in reaching for the thought, and now she has it, and the powerlines spark and burn, shooting through her with revelation, and she falls to the desert floor, she sinks into the silence of the desert floor, and as she does so, she releases Harry from her iron grip, she sinks into the silence of the desert floor, and as she does so, she realizes again that she was wrong, how many times can we be wrong, she wonders? perhaps that is all life amounts to in the end, perhaps being wrong is a sort of reaching for the truth, she was wrong, and now she is light, and she is more than light, she is the desert and all the animals of the desert, and there was no need for her to carry the burden alone, she understands that now, so why had she done so? it was wrong to do that, why had she spent her life carrying so much? and she realizes, too, that she'd wanted to carry the burden, she'd wanted to, how silly she's been, she'd wanted it and wanted it, and now she understands how wrong she was, perhaps that is the thought, the thought she'd been reaching for, the knowledge that no matter what we do we will be wrong, until we reach for the thought, until we cross the desert and touch the light, and she sinks slowly into the red sand, she sinks slowly into the thought, and as she does so, a fox approaches and stares at her, warily, and then he touches his head to hers, and the ground shivers, and the geckos murmur in the distance, and her body returns to her but not what it was, body free of grief, body free of pain, and now she is every fox and scorpion, every grain of sand, and her old self looks about her for something human, but it no longer exists, if it ever did, and she tries one more time to speak, but her voice rasps like sand, and her voice is sand, and her eyes fix open, the eyes of the desert fox, and they will never close again, and her body calls to the animals of the desert, and one by one they come to her, and soon she is every lizard and snake, every hare and ant, the ants that silently gnaw at everything, the ants that never stop moving, never stop pretending, never stop being wrong, and she cradles them all until dawn

# UC San Diego, Medical Center

**tomorrow**'s ox will lead you home, her mother used to say that, and she hasn't understood what it means until now, it means the calm will not begin until the wandering child returns, it means we are our own process, it means she's traced her own steps, and she belongs to her steps now, it means she's redrawn her own lines, and they are crooked, the story of every person is crooked, it means a storm will come in every life and break it, break the body's tender mold, and now she is broken and lying in bed, she's lying in bed in a hospital in San Diego and staring at Julia, she can't believe her darling Julia is here, standing before the window in her room, her darling Julia standing in a white dress, with her black hair falling over her shoulders, and her dark, dark eyes telling her everything will be okay, and she watches as her darling Julia crosses the room to sit, and she listens as Julia pulls out a letter from her purse, she smells her perfume as she shifts in the chair, Guerlain's Vol de Nuit, and she's so happy because her Julia has come to her, her Julia is sitting across from her in her hospital room, pulling a letter from her purse, her darling Julia with the jet black hair falling over her white shoulders, and then she hears her song,

Rachmaninov's Piano Concerto No. 2 in C minor, and she's so happy because she knows her heart has remembered another way to be alive, she's happy because she understands now that the world tells us everything, everything we need to know, but then she turns toward the music and sees Frances, the Talking Mule sitting at the baby grand piano in the corner of her hospital room, opposite Julia, she sees Frances playing her beloved Rachmaninov, and she hates the fact that things fall apart so easily, even now in her hospital room, when she's on death's door, but what really matters? Frances asks her, what really matters? and she looks at him, and then she looks at Julia opening the letter, and she knows, she knows that the most real things and the things we most want look like a dream, and that's okay because she belongs to her steps now, because tomorrow's ox has led her home, and so she laughs, though it hurts to laugh, yes, dreams, even imagination were one way, maybe the only way of attaining oneself, so why grope, why reach, why grasp with a giant hand in the desert, when it's all here, right here, in this hospital room, except she wishes Frances wasn't here, why does he always have to be in the picture, she's never liked him, his arrogance, his way of cutting right to the heart of things, she's redrawn her own lines, and they are crooked, and she doesn't need Frances to cut straight to it, go to hell, she says to him, but he only plays louder, stomping his hoof in time with the Rachmaninov, and there's a place where previous to everything I am, and that's the true place now, she thinks, so why struggle, why worry that Frances is here, too, when there is inside her a place of true light, a place that used to be a dark room with a sphere, but now it is true light, and Julia lives there, too, and Julia is also light, and they are in this hospital room together, it doesn't matter that Frances is here as well, and now Julia is opening the letter, she is reading the letter to her, her darling Julia, with her voice that comes from deep in the forest, her voice that makes her ready to accept her own soul, she is reading to her a letter from the Federal Food and Drug Administration, dated February 27, 1977, she is reading to her with that voice that comes from the forest, dear Ms Hayes, we write to inform you that after years of careful study and research we have come to the conclusion that we must re-examine our policies on health food supplements and baby food, further we have decided to make amendments to the laws governing addition of lead and other substances to the aforementioned supplements and food, we thank you for your letters and your actions as they played a large part in instigating the research that has led to these amendments, sincerely yours, and then Frances picks up the tempo of his hoofing on the floor, and plays with a volume and gusto only he can manage, drowning out the rest of the letter, does anyone tell the truth? he yells over the music, does anyone really believe anything the man ever says? come on Miss Hayes, he says, they're playing you, trying to make you feel good so you'll stop bothering them, that's all, and then he hoofs the linoleum three times for effect, but she doesn't care if it's true or not, she doesn't care anymore if they take the lead out of baby food, out of vitamin supplements, she only cares that Julia is the one sitting in her hospital room, reading her the letter, her darling Julia, sitting there in her white dress with her black hair falling about her shoulders, and her dark, dark eyes, that look at you as if from deep within the forest, just like her voice, a voice that tells her most of our experience comes through pain, most of the journey, the way through the forest, and she knows it's true, even if Frances keeps shouting, does anyone tell the truth? does anyone tell the truth? she knows it's true, and so she rises from her bed, she pulls out the tubes from her nose and the needles from her arms, and she rises from her bed in her hospital gown and goes to Julia, and Julia rises from her chair, and reaches out a hand for her, she reaches out her long arms, she reaches out her long arms and takes Allison in them, and she holds her there in her long arms, and that's when Frances slams down the fallboard on the piano, and he rises, too, and begins spouting all sorts of nonsense, I hope to kiss a duck, you just lost a legal argument to a mule, he stomps his hoofs in anger, o my aching back, we're a team, right? mule and jackass, right? she wants to leave Frances behind, to run to a place where he can never go, but she doesn't know how, and he's so loud, so damn loud, and that's when Julia raises her enormous hand and silences Frances, and she doesn't know how Julia does it, but she doesn't care, because once Julia raises her giant hand, Frances goes mute, and she knows something essential has happened, something essential that isn't meant to be understood, so she doesn't try, she lets Julia hold her in her long arms, and then they're walking together toward the window, and then they're walking out the window and into a forest, and she recognizes the forest as one outside her home in West Virginia, tomorrow's ox will lead you home, her mother used to say, and now she understands what her mother meant, and Julia leads her to a mulberry grove, and Julia plucks the mulberries and feeds them to her, and nothing has ever tasted so good, do you know that life is a question without an answer? Julia asks her, and all she can do is shake her head, because the mulberries taste so good, and the juice drips down her chin, and she doesn't care, she doesn't care if it drips on her hospital gown, or if it stains her fingers, she doesn't care, and Julia touches a finger to her mulberry stained lips, do you know that this is love? she says, and again all Allison can do is nod her head and taste the mulberry juice as it drips down her throat, and all she can think is that she's standing in a grove of mulberry trees in the forest near her West Virginia home with Julia, and all she can think is that her mother was right, yes, she was right, and then she reaches out her own hand to Julia's lips, and she sees that her own hand is enormous, that it's bigger than the world, and she touches her finger to Julia's lips, and that finger becomes a tree of light in the corner of a dark room, and she knows we carry the dark room with us, always, and that it's okay because the longing for God is God, and the hunger is the cry home, and the sparrow, too, is part of us, and with it we'll never have rest because with it comes hope, and the sparrow settles on the highest branch of the mulberry tree, and Julia feeds her one more berry, and the juice is so fine as it drips down her throat, and she is getting bigger and bigger, and she wonders if it's the mulberry juice that's doing this, but Julia tells her no, she tells her it's the hunger, that all we've got is the hunger, and she keeps growing and growing until she towers above the trees, until she can touch the sky, and at first she's scared because she doesn't want to leave Julia, but Julia tells her it's okay, it will all be okay, and she trusts Julia, she has to trust her, so she tries to believe it, even though it's scary growing this tall, and now she's rising toward the moon, and she has to duck her head or else she'll hit it on the moon, and she keeps growing and growing until the moon is just a stepping stool to the stars, and then she's walking on the stars, yes, she's walking through the night sky on the stars, and she keeps walking until she's tired, and so she lies down among the stars and sleeps for a very long time, sleeps for so long that when she wakes she will be refreshed, when she wakes she'll be free of pain, free of grief, when she wakes, she will wake to a silence so profound not even Frances the Talking Mule will be able to break it, and when she wakes she'll find a mulberry in her pocket, and she'll wonder if it was Julia who put it there

# Playlist

3 One Oh, *I Am Woman*

4 Non Blondes, *What's Up?*

Halle Abadi, *Boytoy*

Christina Aguilera, *Fall In Line*

Tori Amos, *Rasberry Swirl*

Ashnikko, *Invitation, Clitoris! The Musical*

Fiona Apple, *Under the Table, Fetch the Bolt Cutters, Ladies*

Emilie Autumn, *Fight Like a Girl*

Sara Bareilles, *King of Anything*

Courtney Barnett, *Nameless, Faceless*

Beyoncé, *Run the World (Girls)*

Bikini Kill, *Rebel Girl*

Björk, *Hyperballad*

Lola Blanc, *Angry Too*

David Bowie, *Cat People (Putting Out Fire)*

Valerie Broussard, *A Little Wicked*

Dove Cameron, *Breakfast, Boyfriend*

CARYS, *When A Girl*

Chrissy Chlapecka, I'm So Hot

Chopin, *Nocturne Op. 9 No. 2 in E flat major*

Nina Chuba, *I Owe You Nothing*

Cloudy June, *Devil Is A Woman*

dodie, *She*

EMM, *Boys Like You*

Florence + The Machine, *Dream Girl Evil, King*

Lesley Gore, *You Don't Own Me*

Hall & Oates, *Maneater*

PJ Harvey, *50ft Queenie, Me-Jane, Man-Size*

The Highwomen, *Highwomen*

Hole, *Celebrity Skin*

Johnny Hollow, *Bogeyman*

Janet Jackson, *Nasty*

Jax, *Cinderella Snapped*

Kesha, *Woman*

Alicia Keys, *Girl on Fire*

KiNG MALA, *she calls me daddy*

Lady Gaga, *Born This Way*

Le Tigre, *Hot Topic*

Little Destroyer, *Alpha*

Little Mix, *Woman's World, Salute*

MARINA, *Man's World*

Milck, *Quiet*

Janelle Monaé, *Pynk*

No Doubt, *Just a Girl*

Okay Kaya, *Asexual Wellbeing*

Paris Paloma, *as good a reason, labour*

Pink, *U + Ur Hand*

Rachmaninov, *Piano Concerto No. 2 in C minor*

Ma Rainey, *Prove It On Me Blues*

Rat City, *Bad*

Kiki Rockwell, *Harbinger, Burn Your Village, Madeline*

Chappell Roan, *Red Wine Supernova*

Rosalía, *I See a Darkness*

Buffy Sainte-Marie, *It's My Way*

Rina Sawayama, *This Hell*

Shakira, *She Wolf*

Nina Simone, *Ain't No Use, Wild is the Wind, Sinnerman*

SkyDxddy, *Pretty Distraction*

Sonic Youth, *Kool Thing*

Hailee Steinfeld, *Most Girls*

Sister Rosetta Tharpe, *Strange Things Happening Every Day*

Tubes, *Attack of the Fifty Foot Woman*

twst, *Sugared Up*

Gin Wigmore, *Kill Of The Night*

Hannah Williams and The Affirmations, *Fifty Foot Woman*

Hayley Williams, *Simmer*

Xana, *Goddess*

PETER GRANDBOIS is the author of fourteen books, most recently *Domestic Bestiary*. His poems, stories, and essays have appeared in over one hundred and fifty journals. His plays have been nominated for several New York Innovative Theatre Awards and have been performed in St. Louis, Columbus, Los Angeles, and New York. He is poetry editor at Boulevard magazine and teaches at Denison University in Ohio. You can find him at www.petergrandbois.com

Irena Dubrovna is the fictional protagonist of both the 1942 film *Cat People*, directed by Jacques Tourneur, and the 1982 film, directed by Paul Schrader (though in the Schrader film her name was changed to *Irena Gallier*). She is of Serbian descent. This is her first novel.

www.ingramcontent.com/pod-product-compliance
Lightning Source LLC
Chambersburg PA
CBHW010608310726
48969CB00010B/2608